A. L. TIPPETT

A
DRAGON'S
MIND

THE MINATH CHRONICLES
BOOK 1

CW00656728

Copyright © 2020 A. L. Tippett

All rights reserved. This book or parts thereof may not be reproduced in
any form, stored in any retrieval system, or transmitted in any form by any
means–electronic, mechanical, photocopy, recording, or otherwise–without
prior written permission of the publisher.

This is a work of fiction. Names, places, characters and incidents are either
the product of the author's imagination or are used fictitiously, and any
resemblance to any actual persons, living or dead, organizations, locales or
events is entirely coincidental.

Ebook ISBN: 978-0-6488121-1-1
Paperback ISBN: 978-0-6488121-0-4
Cover designed by MiblArt
Published by FireFly Books

FIRE FLY
BOOKS

British spelling and grammar used throughout this book

CONTENTS

CHAPTER ONE

SLINKING FORWARD, SERAPHINA AZURA stalked her prey. The fresh mountain air filled her lungs as she peered through the trees, seeking her quarry. Sweat beaded on her temple and dripped down her neck while her shirt clung to her tanned skin. Her backpack, which felt heavier by the hour, made her sweat even more. Glancing down, Sera tracked the deer, the two-toed hoof prints obvious in the mud. The ground was soft here. Being careful not to slip she sidled quietly behind a large boulder to consider her next move. There was a fresh-water creek not far ahead. Chances were good the deer was headed that way and she could cut it off before it reached the water. She swung her rifle out of the sling on her pack, slid the magazine into place and pulled the bolt back, ready to load the first bullet.

Closing her sapphire eyes, she listened intently. The quiet of the bush swept all her worries away as she tuned into the sounds around her. The rustle of the wind through the trees, the chatter of the native birds, and the cheerful bubbling of the nearby creek enveloped her. It was so much calmer than the busy streets of her home in Mandar City. Her job as a Tracker at the Mythic Relations Office kept her busy travelling around the country so, thankfully, she didn't have to spend too much time holed up in her tiny apartment. Whenever she had a weekend off from work, she liked to escape into the wilderness to do some traditional hunting. It was her preferred way to relax, as opposed to the usual stress of tracking and reporting the movements of mythical creatures that had broken the law.

The rustle of leaves underfoot alerted her to the deer's location just ahead of her and to the east. Opening her eyes, she silently lifted the gun and laid her right cheek against the stock. Lining up the deer's head in her sights, she inhaled, held her breath and gently squeezed the trigger.

The sun's last rays bled away into the west; she'd have to make camp soon and the creek was as good a place as any to settle for the night. After pulling the long tendrils of auburn hair that had escaped from her ponytail back into place, she slid her favourite knife through the belly of the doe she'd shot and deftly skinned the animal. The hide was of good quality and a rich red, a popular colour. She'd be able to fetch a decent price for it at the Mandar City Market. After sectioning the meat, making sure she kept a portion aside for tonight's meal, she salted the rest of it and hung it in a burlap sack off a low-hanging tree branch. She didn't want the meat to spoil before she made it back to civilisation. She cleaned her hunting knife and warmth filled her heart at the memory of her father gifting the blade to her at her graduation from MINATH. The Mandar Institute for Negotiators, Alchemists, Trackers and Hunters offered four-year apprenticeships in each of their four programmes for five recruits a year. Knowing how much it meant to her father, she was thrilled to be chosen as one of the five Tracker apprentices when she turned seventeen. He had been so proud when she graduated as a fully qualified Tracker like him.

The short blade had belonged to her mother and was perfect both for skinning and close combat. The staghorn handle moulded itself to her hand as if it had been made specifically for her. Arms training at MINATH included all types of weapons and whilst her rifle was practical when hunting larger game, she preferred knives. She named her knife Firinne, and it had a pattern of silver running along its edge. An Alchemist had assisted the blacksmith in the forging of the blade, and it was inlaid with the essence of numerous crystals to battle a variety of magical creatures.

Her calloused hands pawed briskly through the contents of her pack. She shifted the small tub of Heal ointment out of the way and pulled out her water canteen. Making her way towards the creek, Sera enjoyed the tranquillity of the water bubbling over the stones and the lilting birdsong as they heralded the demise of another day. Picking her way carefully over the mossy rocks, she bent down and picked some watercress that hugged the bank. She quickly refilled the canteen and squeezed two drops of the Filter treatment she always kept in her pack into the water. The Alchemists at the MRO worked tirelessly to create various treatments to be used in the field by Trackers and Hunters. The vial of Filter ensured that any water they found whilst away from the city was safe to drink. All Trackers and Hunters carried an MRO Survival Kit issued by the Alchemists on their assignments. They also had the option to request additional treatments they needed for specific tasks. Sera remembered one particularly cold mission during winter where she had to stake out the den of a rogue snow foxen that had killed a child. She had been thankful for the tonic of Warmth an alchemist had made for her as she shivered her way through two nights, making notes on the mythic's habits.

Sera smiled to herself. While the alchemists may be talented, they weren't known for their creativity when it came to naming the mixtures, although their sensible names did make it easy to remember what they were all used for. Tucking the Filter bottle securely back in its place, she swiftly made camp to beat the approaching dusk. After setting the fire alight and laying her bed roll out, she glanced at her mobile phone, noting the one measly bar of service that shone in the top corner. She turned it off. She wouldn't need her phone tonight.

As she lay in her bedroll, Sera drowsily gazed through the tree's leafy canopy into the night sky. Her belly was full, from the watercress she'd found in the creek along with the fresh venison she'd cooked over the fire that now flickered beside her. The stars peppering the blackness and the moon's thin silver crescent gave little light. She always enjoyed her camping trips away by herself. No need to check in every night by phone with her Hunter partner, no need to write a report every day on the movements of the beast she was tracking. Her body was exhausted from the hard trek today, the dull ache settling into her muscles. Letting herself relax, she slipped into unconsciousness.

CHAPTER TWO

THAT NIGHT, SHE DREAMT. She felt the resistance of the air as her strong, copper coloured wings pulled her through the sky. The ground was far away, but the sliver of moon was her close friend. Her ivory claws curled in anticipation of the hunt and she knew that the lethal horns and spikes adorning her scaled skull weren't necessary to defeat the puny game that roamed these hills. The beating of her glorious wings was a familiar and yet entirely foreign sensation. She suddenly realised she wasn't alone. She swung her head to and fro, searching for the imposter when she realised the other consciousness wasn't outside at all, but rather inside her mind. With that realisation came a violent mental attack. She recoiled, desperately trying to evade the internal ambush. Scenting the air, she smelt smoke from a fire. She scanned the ground far below and saw the red glow of dying embers to the south. Folding her wings, she dived towards the enemy.

Gasping, Sera bolted upright in her bedroll, drenched in sweat. Looking around she saw the coals still glowed from her fire.

What a strange dream. She still felt the elation inside her chest as she relived the feeling of freedom and power from her flight. Blinking the sleep from her eyes she shook her head, trying to dispel the remnants of the dream from her thoughts, but pressure built in her eardrums and she recognised the sound of heavy wing beats, getting louder with every stroke. The limited light from the moon vanished as the dark shadow of giant wings filled the sky above her.

Eyes wide, Sera felt a scream clawing up her throat, but she forced it down. Wrenching free from her bedding, she scrambled for her rifle. In one move she swung the gun up and threw herself at the nearest tree, balancing against it to steady her shaking arms. Branches snapped and tree trunks cracked as the giant beast roared its anger. Leaves and dust ballooned around her, making her cough as the creature landed. Sera struggled to shove the bolt into position, but fear made her fingers clumsy and wooden. She glanced back up at the gaping maw and froze, unable to pull the trigger as she stared at the creature in front of her. It was a dragon. Her eyes saw the dragon, but her brain couldn't process it. There weren't supposed to be any dragons left. The Trackers and Hunters of old had hunted them to extinction during the Mythic War. Before she could snap out of her daze, the emerald eyes of the dragon were upon her, pinning her to the spot.

Time seemed to slow as they locked eyes. Sera flashed back to reading a story in her history class when she was studying to be a Tracker. The tale of Borin and The Sapphire Dragon. Borin was a famous Tracker from before the Mythic War who had found a rogue sapphire dragon. The female dragon had hypnotised Borin, compelling him to protect her. Instead of contacting his Hunter partner as per procedure, her magic forced him to run away with her. Rumour had it that he shared top secret information with the dragon and endangered the citizens of Mandar. Borin's partner, the Hunter Ajax, had tracked them into the mountains and tried to talk sense into them. With Borin's loyalties divided, the Sapphire Dragon then murdered the Tracker in cold blood. Hunter Ajax carried out the law by executing the rogue dragon then and there. Sera could just recall a paragraph in the story when Borin first met the dragon: he had dropped his weapons, bowed down and avoided eye contact which was why the dragon had spared his life. She wrenched her eyes away from the penetrating orbs staring at her and threw herself on the ground. She made sure to drop her gun to the ground to appear unarmed but kept it within reach in case she needed it.

The dragon peered down at her prone form and snaked its head forward, "Stand up and speak, human," the deep voice commanded. "Why were you intruding on my thoughts?"

Her mind boggled. Not only was there a flesh and blood dragon standing in front of her, but it could speak! She didn't know if her colleagues would ever believe her when she reported this mythic encounter.

A low growl rumbled from deep within the dragon's belly and he repeated, "Stand up! Why did you connect with me?"

Keeping her eyes down, Sera frowned as she stood on shaking legs. *What does he mean, intruding in his mind?* Aloud, she murmured, "I don't know what you mean."

He huffed a frustrated sigh and smoke curled from his nostrils. "Earlier this evening, you entered my mind and observed my flight before I realised you were there. I did not welcome you and allow your conscious to join with mine, and yet, there you were. How and why?"

Shaking her head in disbelief, Sera managed to stammer out, "I thought it was a dream. I don't know how it happened."

His tail whipped around and felled a nearby sapling, frightening her. "You don't know how it happened?" He eyed her incredulously. "You have no idea of your power? It's either that, or you're lying. Whichever one, it is... troublesome. I see no alternative but to seize you until we understand what danger you may pose."

He acted so fast she didn't have a chance to reach for her gun; his left talon snapped forward and sharp claws locked around her body before he leapt into the air. Three powerful strokes of his wings saw them above the tree line. Sera couldn't help herself, she screamed and beat her hands against his claws in a futile escape attempt. She gazed in anguish as her pack, with her weapons, ointments and her phone dropped out of sight, and with it her hopes of escape. The wind whistled past her ears and the cold air tore at her clothes. She felt dizzy as the earth grew smaller, her camp near the creek no longer distinguishable from the rest of the bush. The dragon banked to the west, towards a dark shadow on the horizon, barely distinguishable from the night sky. Straining her eyes, she made it out to be a distant mountain that rose high into the sky, dwarfing everything else. It made the ranges she'd been climbing earlier that day seem little more than hills.

They travelled quickly, his great wings torpedoing them through the sky. She was unsure exactly how much ground they had covered but knew it would have taken her weeks to hike on foot. Peering down, she saw they were flying across the Red Waste, a seemingly endless stretch of dead land, a remnant of the horror of the Mythic War. The years of fighting had stained the land beneath them red with blood, and it could no longer support life. No trees or rivers graced the terrain, and no animals dared tread on the lifeless earth.

Where, in the name of Ghaia, am I being taken? Even invoking the Goddess of Earth's name could not stop the fear from coiling itself around Sera's gut, taking fierce hold of her sanity. Various scenarios sprouted unbidden into her mind of ways she would be killed by the beast. As time wore on, her body started to stiffen from the freezing air, her limbs protesting from being tightly confined within the dragon's iron grip. After what seemed like an age had passed, but in reality would have been no more than a few hours, a long, thin, silver shimmer on the mountainside caught her eye. As they flew closer, she saw it was a waterfall reflecting the moon's light. Sera couldn't locate where it ended but she saw that it exited the mountain from a gaping hole near the top of a cliff face. The dragon seemed to be heading straight for it. His weight shifted and his wings changed their rhythm as he prepared to land inside the mouth of the cave. He gained purchase on the edge with his hind legs and dropped his weight forward, jolting her as three of his legs took their combined weight. He held her upright now, using his hind legs to walk further into the cave and his right foreleg for balance.

Her heart hammered and panic set in – feverishly she searched for an escape route in the hope that she could make a quick getaway. She knew from what she'd read in the past that dragons ate meat, but the fact that he hadn't killed her immediately gave her hope he wasn't planning on making her his next meal. She didn't want to take any chances, though. From what she could see the main source of light shone from the cave mouth, but there seemed to be small pinpricks of light high above her head as well. While she was craning her neck back, a smouldering light appeared above her head as the dragon's chest glowed and a deep rumble echoed around them. He opened his jaws and breathed flames onto a pile of logs in the centre of the cave. She cringed away from the blast of heat. Turning quickly, he carried her to the wall of the cavern where part of a skeleton of some great beast sat, not as large as the dragon but still bigger than any other animal she'd ever seen. The spine of the creature lay on the floor with the ribs pointing towards the ceiling. With large stalagmites at each end of the ribcage closing off the gaps, it created a very effective cage.

He adjusted his grip on her, dangled her through the hole where the sternum should be and dropped her inside. She stumbled and fell as she landed, her muscles numb and ungainly from being held so tightly in the frigid air for so long. Her teeth chattered uncontrollably, and while her jacket had offered some protection from the wind, she was still freezing. With the fire crackling before them, Sera began to thaw out and could finally see the layout of her new prison. With her back to the wall, the cave's entry was to her left, where thin green vines crawled along the rock. Beyond the fire was the stream that tumbled into the waterfall she'd seen as they had flown in. She could just make out a cluster of boulders on the far side of the cave where the stream emerged from a small, dark void. She could barely distinguish the ceiling of the cave that faded into the darkness far above her head. Shadows danced on the stalagmites and stalactites scattered through the massive space.

The dragon stalked away from her, his tail swinging, and began pacing the floor. The light from the fire created a golden sheen on his coppery scales that covered a muscular body. As he walked past her, Sera saw a jagged scar running across his left shoulder. It must have been a great beast that tore through the scales and into his hide as this dragon was obviously in his prime. His immense form struck her once again; she wouldn't be able to touch his belly even if she stood on her tiptoes. The fact that he fit inside this cave comfortably went to show just how colossal the space was. As he turned away from the cave mouth, his green eyes flicked to hers and he stopped his march.

His imposing figure leaned over her as his claws dug grooves into the rocky ground. "What is your name, human?"

"Seraphina. But everyone just calls me Sera."

His eyes sharpened for a moment while he considered her. "Interesting. And where do you come from?"

"Mandar City." If she could keep him talking, maybe he wouldn't eat her and she could keep working on an escape plan. "I work at the Mythic Relations Office."

He snorted. "Doing what, may I ask?"

"I'm a Tracker. My job is to track down mythical creatures who have broken the law and report their position back to the Mythic Relations Office. Depending on the crime they either send a Negotiator to speak with them or a Hunter to…" she trailed off, unsure if she should finish the sentence given the position she was in.

"I know what a Hunter does." He dismissed her explanation with a flick of his tail. She could almost hear the eye roll in his tone. "At least you're a Tracker. Those Hunters from the MRO are utterly intolerable. They are far too arrogant for their own good."

"You know about the MRO?" She had figured that if her workplace didn't know dragons still existed, then dragons wouldn't know about the Mythic Relations Office.

"Of course," he sneered. "You all seem to think that you know what is best for this world when you're the ones throwing off the balance."

"That's not fair," she said with a scowl. "We do important work, keeping the lines of communication open and relationships friendly between all magical creatures and the human race."

"Really? Is that what you truly believe? Oh dear. And how do you think our relationship is going?" he asked with a raised eyebrow.

Frowning, Sera opened her mouth to respond but then closed it, unable to find a fitting retort. No one had ever trained her to deal with a dragon's sharp tongue.

Stretching his wings, he strode away from her towards the mouth of the cave. "They really have shrouded the truth in a pretty lie. We will speak more after I have returned from the hunt."

With that, he spread his wings and leapt into the air, dropping out of sight. He reappeared a few moments later, covered in the silvery moonlight, and flew east before vanishing behind the cloud. She was finally alone.

CHAPTER THREE

~FOUR WEEKS AGO~

SERA'S STEPS QUICKENED AS she eagerly made her way to the stables to meet Balthazar. Three times a week Sera would meet with the unicorn for a combination of endurance and combat training. He was a buckskin stallion and a great warrior. There had been a few incidences in Sera's short Tracking career where she had stumbled upon an aggressive wild animal whilst on a mission and Balthazar had saved her life by skewering the beast. However, he did like to make sure she knew how much she was in his debt.

"Hey Balthazar, how goes the war?" Sera grinned at the unicorn.

"Poorly," he huffed. "Those damnable colts think they know everything. I've been asked to teach them some manners, but I swear to Ghaia, the next one to try and nip me will spend the next ten years ploughing the field."

"You're a grumpy old thing today, aren't you?" she teased, scratching his wither.

He snorted at her and shook his black mane in agitation.

"Come on, it's endurance training today, and I need to get away from these jerks," she said and tightened his girth.

"As do I," was his wry response as she leapt onto his back. Once she was settled, he set off at a steady trot away from the stables and the peculiarly sweet smell of manure.

Following the Mythic War much infrastructure had been destroyed, including the factories that built vehicles. They were recovering slowly – certain government officials had access to the few cars and helicopters produced since the war – but resources were thin, and their attention had been dedicated to the production of fresh water, food and shelter first. To combat the lack of vehicles available, the MRO had made a treaty with the wild unicorns that roamed the countryside. Their services were required as a means of transport when Trackers or Hunters needed to travel long distances in rough country to find rogues. They were also handy with their horn in a tight spot. In return, they were offered stables, feed and protection from the werewolves that still hunted them in the wilds. They were finicky beasts, demanding respect from their riders. They allowed a saddle and bridle to be worn for the comfort of the rider but flatly refused to accept a bit in their mouth. When the Trackers and Hunters graduated from MINATH and commenced employment with the MRO, they were partnered with a unicorn. There was never any problem matching the riders with their mounts, as the unicorns would make the decisions for themselves. That didn't mean the unicorns always made the right choice, but they would never admit that themselves.

Following the fence line, Sera and Balthazar travelled briskly, past the building that housed the Mythic Relations Office and out onto the main road out of town. She nodded to one of the Negotiators, Aaron, who was on his phone outside the office. Sweat rolled down his ebony forehead as he argued the case of a rogue mythic to a Hunter. Negotiators acted like counsellors and helped rehabilitate creatures that had started down the wrong path. If it was their first offence and the crime wasn't too serious, the Negotiator would take them on as a patient and help them get back on the right path. This was usually through a combination of therapy sessions and volunteering in the local community. Aaron lifted a hand in silent greeting and continued his dispute. A small sigh of frustration escaped her lips.

"Come now, Seraphina," her unicorn coaxed her. "Speak to me. What has happened that has caused you to, once again, label your colleagues as jerks?"

"Aside from the fact that none of them gave me the time of day during my apprenticeship? And then did a complete one-eighty when Tyler chose me as his partnered Tracker?"

"Yes. Aside from all that. We have previously discussed at length their idiotic need to conform. We don't need to go over it again."

"That's true. But I'm always keen to criticise them some more."

"Don't wallow, Seraphina. It's unbecoming," he reproached.

"Gods, don't you sound old-fashioned today?" She sniggered.

"And now you're deflecting." He flicked his tail hard enough for the end of it to swing up and sting her on the thigh.

"Hey! You did that on purpose!"

He snorted and shook his head. "I don't know what you mean. There was a fly."

She poked her tongue out at the back of his head before dropping her shoulders in defeat. She whispered, "I can't stand him."

"Hunter Tyler?"

"Yes."

Balthazar cocked a sympathetic ear back towards her. "What happened?"

Letting go of the reins, Sera wrapped her arms around her middle. "He thinks he owns everyone. Including me."

"How so?"

"I... I don't know if I can find the right words. The way he speaks to me... it makes me feel physically ill. I go out of my way to avoid him at work. He makes me feel... unsafe. I don't trust him. If I can't trust my Hunter, who can I trust?"

"You can trust me," Balthazar offered.

She leaned forward to hug his neck, burying her face in his mane, and mumbled, "Thank goodness I have you."

He nickered to her and turned his head to nudge her boot.

The gentle sway of his walk eased her troubled thoughts as they made their way through the farmer's fields in companionable silence. There were still many buildings, particularly on the outskirts of the city, that were dilapidated. Damaged from the Mythic War, the government had condemned the older houses and left them to rot. Sera always felt a pang of sadness when they rode past the broken structures. So many families had lost loved ones in the war and then, to add insult to injury, had lost their homes when they couldn't afford to fix them.

The stifling heat of the day made her green uniform cling to her, and Balthazar's creamy coat already had a sheen of sweat on it. Sera kept the reins loose, he didn't need her to add to his discomfort, and they both knew where they were going today. The ocean was only a half hour's ride from the stables and would offer a perfect place to work on their stamina together. The ride there was a great warm-up for them both and gave them the chance to talk. Whenever the Trackers and their unicorns weren't away on a mission for the MRO, they were required to train together throughout the week.

As they approached the coast, they passed a black lynx. The lynx sat down on his haunches and watched, unblinking, as they trotted past. Small dark flames licked around his neck like a mane before following his spine down to his tail where the fire flared at the tip. She raised a hand in greeting and it blinked once. Sera shrugged it off; in her experience, most of the feline mythics were aloof. The ocean glimmered ahead of them, like a precious jewel reflecting the sun's rays. She inhaled the crisp scent of the sea air, the slight stickiness of the salt coating her face. The wind whispered through the sand reeds, their spiky heads nodding to the sun.

Sera kept her torso flexible and moved with Balthazar as he left the farmlands behind them and slipped cautiously down onto the dunes. He had to be careful not to canter through the soft sand, as even magical creatures could tear their muscles. They made it to the harder sand where he wasn't at risk of damaging any tendons and she swung off his back. Small waves folded onto the shoreline and made for a peaceful ambience. Sera eyed the ocean distrustfully; no matter how serene it appeared she knew the dangers that lurked beneath the surface. So long as they didn't run into any kraken or seahorses, she'd consider it a successful training day.

Balthazar followed her gaze, then nudged her shoulder. "Don't fret, I can handle anything that comes out of the water."

"If you say so." She shrugged. No use worrying about it until it happened.

Together, they started their training session, her jogging beside the unicorn's striking figure. He was the stuff of every little girl's dreams, his long, black tail swinging with each powerful stride, his mane rippling in the ocean breeze. But it was Balthazar's horn that was the most awe-inspiring thing about him. It was hard as diamond and longer than her forearm. Onyx stones encircled the base of the obsidian horn, and while Balthazar refused to tell her their purpose, she was certain she had seen them glowing during battle.

Sand flicked up and coated his flanks as he galloped ahead of her, pushing his limits. She switched between running and jogging, giving her body time to recover between sprints. Staying alert, she kept a close eye on the shallows. Balthazar returned from his gallop, blowing hard, but within minutes had regained his composure.

"Ready to surf?" She grinned at him.

He rolled his brown eyes and snorted at her. "Has anyone ever told you how strange you are, even for a human?"

"Not in so many words." She bumped his shoulder with her elbow, enjoying his easy companionship.

Sand surfing was her favourite part of their training regime. She pulled the small fibreglass board from where it was folded up on the back of the saddle and clicked the catch to release it. It sprung open to four times its size in an oval shape, at which point she placed it on the ground. She clipped the long reins onto a buckle at the back of the saddle and ran them back to the board. Balthazar leant down to the board and tapped it with his horn, creating a protective ward around the front of it. This would stop her getting a mouthful of the sand that would be kicked up by his hooves when they were galloping. She patted the unicorn on the rump before picking up the reins and stepping onto the board.

"Ready when you are, Balthazar."

He eased into a walk, and the board jerked forward under Sera's weight as she used the reins to balance. He jumped into a trot and she leant back slightly to keep the board under her feet. He tossed a quick look over his shoulder to check that she was still upright before leaping into a canter.

She kept her core strong and held onto the reins. The pounding of Balthazar's hooves kept a steady rhythm as the board slid easily over the wet sand. Grinning, Sera leant right and scooted the board closer to the ocean. She could barely call it exercise when it was this much fun. Even though she would have sore arms and abs tomorrow, it was worth it for the adrenaline. It was a great way for them to use each other's strength to improve their own. Pulling her weight behind him whilst cantering on the beach helped Balthazar to further develop his stamina, while she worked on her upper body. A wild laugh bubbled up from Sera's belly as the wind whipped through the ward and tangled her hair. Any sand that flew into the ward slid off to the side as it hit the invisible barrier. They both were sprayed by ocean mist from the wave crests as they crashed onto the coast. Together they flew along the shoreline until they arrived at the rocky cliffs that blocked them from going further. Balthazar bent his hocks and dropped his rump low into a sliding stop, forcing Sera to leap from the board to avoid catapulting into him. She tried to take a few running steps to slow her forward momentum but failed. As she fell, she tucked herself into a ball and managed an ungainly forward roll back up onto her feet.

Panting, Sera dusted the sand off her clothes and raised an eyebrow at Balthazar. "What was that for?"

The unicorn chuffed a few times in his version of a laugh. "Just keeping you on your toes. You've got to be ready for anything." He snorted at her, covering her arm in dirt and mucous from his nostrils.

"Gross. You know I hate it when you do that." Sera screwed up her nose in disgust as she wiped off the scum on her tank top.

"You should be delighted that a unicorn as majestic as myself has deigned to share my mucous with a human such as yourself."

"Has anyone ever told you how strange you are, even for a unicorn?" she deadpanned, using his own words against him.

He chuffed at her once more. She chuckled along with him. Turning back towards the cliffs, they stepped up onto the rocky plateau at their base. Rockpools were exposed with a colourful array of life inhabiting the tiny pools. Electric blue starfish and vibrant purple crabs clung to the slippery walls while the silvery flash of tiny fish caught Sera's eye as they darted undercover. Sera knelt to get a closer look. She loved observing the miniature ecosystems. As she leaned over, she felt the ground beneath her shift unnaturally. She leapt away blindly, splashing into the water, and pulled her knife from its sheath. The boulder she had been standing on rose up, cracking as it broke away from the rest of the stony outcrop. It wasn't a boulder. Three pairs of spindly legs held up the armoured body, and large pincers clicked out from under the exoskeleton. Two long, segmented tails swung up threateningly.

"Shit! Balthazar, watch out for the scorpius!" she yelled.

This mythic was a master of camouflage and deceptively nimble. It wielded heavy clubs at the end of both its tails. The armoured back was almost as high as her shoulder, but the tails made it appear even taller. The scorpius whirled around and aimed a strike towards her torso. Dropping to the ground, she rolled to the side to evade the twin blows. The scrape of the rough rock bit unforgivingly into her skin. Chips of rock exploded beside her as the hammers struck the ground. She was a Tracker, not a Hunter. Much better equipped for hiding and finding traces of rogue mythics than open combat, it was still mandatory that she undergo some Hunter training for this exact scenario.

The MINATH mantra, "Capture, don't kill," echoed in her mind as she tried to find a pattern in the mythic's movements.

She heard Balthazar whinny behind her, but she couldn't spare him a look. Keeping her eyes trained on the creature she twirled Firinne between her fingers, using the familiar feel to help her focus, and searched for an opening. There was meant to be a small nodule in their armour in the centre of their abdomen. If she managed to hit the nub hard enough, it should become paralysed for half an hour, allowing her time to detain it.

Assuming it doesn't club me to death while I'm trying to give it a belly rub.

The scorpius scuttled swiftly towards her, readying its heavy weapon for another attack. Concentrating on avoiding the deadly cudgels, she almost forgot about the pincers. A claw the size of her arm darted forward and barely missed her throat as she threw herself out of the way. Stumbling upright, she felt the blossom of blood dampen her shirt. The scorpius had missed her neck but sliced into her bicep. Hissing in pain, Sera stumbled backwards to get out of its range.

If I have to kill it to save myself, I will.

The thought of taking her first mythic life made her stomach clench, but if it was a case of kill or be killed, she'd prefer to do the killing. The creature scurried forward, taking advantage of her misstep, tails raised as it prepared to smash into her body.

"Balthazar!" Her voice crept up an octave.

The unicorn was already there. He double-barrelled the mythic's plated body with his hind legs, and while it didn't damage the armour, it did flip the creature onto its back. Sera seized the opportunity and vaulted onto its bared belly, plunging the hilt of Firinne onto its Achilles heel. The staghorn handle found its mark and, after a moment of resistance, the bump clicked down. The desperate scrabbling of the scorpius' legs immediately froze and its body stiffened. Adrenaline still poured through her body as she slackened her tense hold on the knife. Pushing herself off the underbelly of the paralysed mythic, she staggered over to Balthazar.

She leant her head against his and whispered, "Thank you."

"All in a day's work," was his gruff reply. But he followed it up with a soft whicker and snuffled her hair with his muzzle. "That's five times I have saved your life now. I'm winning."

Her heart rate slowing to a more reasonable rate, she flicked her long braid over her shoulder and flashed a cheeky grin. "I'm pretty sure I distracted him so you could save me, and I did incapacitate him... so I think we're even."

The unicorn stamped his hoof. "You wouldn't have been able to paralyse it if it wasn't for my help. You would be a mushed-up pile of muscle and bone by now. I win."

Laughing, Sera lightly cuffed him. "Fine, fine, you win, you sensitive old horse."

"Take that back." The unicorn's eyes turned black and his horn sparked with magic.

Throwing her hands in the air, she struggled to keep a straight face as she said, "Sorry! I'm sorry. You're not a horse. You're the most amazing, fantastic mythic I am honoured to call my friend and saviour." As Balthazar relaxed and his magic quelled, she added in a quiet aside, "Who has a superiority complex."

He swung his head toward her, ears back, glaring. "What did you say?"

"Nothing. Just ruminating on my supreme inferiority to you, oh great one."

"Harumph." He stomped away from her, tail swishing, his hooves striking the rocky ground a little harder than usual.

Sighing, Sera pulled her phone out and made a call. The MRO would want to pick up the scorpius before it regained control of its body and take it to the Iniques Rehabilitation Centre. And she'd have to write a situation report on the scuffle.

CHAPTER FOUR

SOMEONE WAS WATCHING HER. Sera's eyes shot open and she bolted upright. Morning sunlight streamed into the cavern, highlighting the bright green eyes that stared back at her. She had hoped for a moment upon waking that yesterday was a bad dream. Adrenaline rushed through her veins as the previous day's events flooded her mind. The dragon had curled up in front of her cage and was watching her intently. Even lying down, his bulky form made her heart hammer in fright. She tried to take deep breaths as she scooted as far away from him as she could. Automatically she reached for her blade at her hip and swore quietly when she remembered she'd taken her belt off when she made camp. The dragon's eyes glimmered in what appeared to be amusement, and he blew some smoke in her direction.

"Do not fear. I don't intend to harm you."

That was all very well for him to say, but all the old stories had dragons painted as devious and cunning, always ready with a lie. She couldn't trust him. But that wasn't her biggest concern right now. Her bladder was protesting loudly, drowning out the voice in her head screaming to run away. She wasn't sure she was so desperate yet that she was willing to soil her new abode, especially in front of the dragon. Unsure how to explain her need for a bathroom break, and confident he wouldn't grant her one anyway, she awkwardly stood up. Cocking his head, the dragon scrutinised her.

"I suppose you are in need of relief?" He rose and walked away.

Confused, she watched as he disappeared behind a large boulder at the back of the cave.

It appears there may be more to this giant hole than meets the eye.

The dragon returned quickly, clasping something small between two claws. He gently pushed some sort of shiny pot through an opening between the ribs towards her. Eyeing him warily she shuffled closer and saw it was a bedpan.

That was considerate of him. She quickly stamped that thought out. Everyone knew dragons weren't thoughtful. He would demand something from her in return. She would have to be careful.

"Better than nothing." She shrugged casually, trying not to show her fear. With the vain hope that it might lead to him letting her go, she added, "Thank you." It couldn't hurt to be polite and appeal to his kinder side. *If it exists.*

"You are welcome. I will leave you in peace and return shortly." With that, he retreated behind the rock at the back of the cave once again and left her alone with her full bladder.

A dragon. There is a very real dragon. There is a very real, very dangerous dragon that has taken me captive.

Her breath hitched as hysteria threatened to set in. Pushing against the panic, she closed her eyes and imagined she was home in her apartment with her flatmate, Hazel. She could almost smell the aroma of the coffee that Hazel roasted for them every morning without fail. They would then sit down on the couch in comfortable silence and watch the news on the TV together, before beginning their working day at the MRO; Sera as a Tracker, Hazel as an Alchemist. She was a pale, willowy girl, with dark brown hair and glasses and had been in the same year as Sera at MINATH. She was one of the few people who hadn't shied away from befriending her. The other eighteen apprentices had always given her sideways glances and whispered behind her back.

They always treated me as an outsider. I don't understand why... I would have been happy to share the lessons my father taught me. Their attitudes had transformed when Tyler chose her as his Tracker. Her lip automatically lifted in a sneer as she contemplated her Hunter. A bully at heart, he enjoyed using his natural charm to persuade people to follow his lead.

At least she'd had Hazel. The four years of training would have been utter hell without her one friend.

If only Hazel were here now.

Always logical, Hazel would have had plenty of theories as to what Sera should do to escape. If she couldn't figure it out, she would research until she had a plan. Sera could only hope that her flatmate would report her missing soon, but she'd probably be eaten by the damned dragon before a search party would be sent out. She couldn't rely on a rescue team to save her.

I have to figure out a way to save myself.

Channelling her inner Hazel, Sera methodically pushed against each of the ribs that made up her prison, hoping to find a weak link so she could flee while the dragon was gone. Admittedly, she didn't know how to get out of the cave yet, but she intended to tackle her escape plan one step at a time. If she focused on the big picture too much she would become overwhelmed. Fear would take over reason, destroying any chance of making it out alive. There didn't seem to be any movement in the bony structures so she couldn't break out that way. They were too close together for her to be able to slip between them. The stalagmites that bookended the ribcage were smooth; there was no way to climb them. The gap above her head where the sternum once lay was more than twice her height, she couldn't reach it even if she jumped. There wasn't a thing in her prison that she could use as a tool to break out – no rocks, no rope, nothing.

She thought of her father, of Hazel, of Balthazar. They wouldn't have even noticed she was missing yet. It was typical for her to go off the radar for a few days when she went on a solo camping trip. They wouldn't be expecting her home for another two nights. She was good at her job, and loved tracking, even with the risk that came with it. To think she had fallen into danger on what was meant to be a harmless way to earn some extra cash.

Her adrenaline spiked and the panic she'd been holding at bay crashed over her like a wave. Screaming, she charged at the bones with the vague hope the impact of her body hitting them would crack one.

I have to get out of here. I can't just sit down and wait to die. I have to do SOMETHING!

She ran again and again into the bars that imprisoned her. She eventually had to stop, her body protesting loudly. A sheen of sweat covered her, with bruises peppering her biceps and collarbones. She sat down with a huff, defeated. The adrenaline that had been coursing through her veins dissipated with the departure of the dragon, and now she was just exhausted. She hadn't been asleep for long in her bedroll before he appeared and she had already been tired from her hike that day. If only she had her backpack, she would have her phone to call for help and tools to escape.

"If wishes were fishes..." she muttered aloud and yawned. The fog that now clouded her brain wasn't going anywhere without some sleep, so Sera decided to rest while she could and make a plan later with a clear mind. Lying on the uneven floor she did her best to get comfortable. The constant burble of the stream that wound through the cave offered a soothing ambience. Closing her eyes, she slowed her breathing and let her body relax. Exhaustion quickly won out and she fell into the black oblivion of sleep.

CHAPTER FIVE

THE AFTERNOON SUN'S RAYS that seeped through the fissures in the cave's ceiling reflected off the stream, creating dancing patterns on the walls. The daylight revealed more of the cave's details to her, but not enough to offer any hope of an easy escape. She unconsciously reached for her knife at her waist, only to remember it was still with her backpack at the campsite. She often found it easier to focus her mind when she ran her fingers along the staghorn handle. Without Firinne in its sheath, it felt like she was missing a part of herself. She sighed.

The only unknowns are that giant boulder the dragon disappeared behind and the entry hole of the stream. If I can only get out of this ribcage I can check them out.

Interrupting her planning, the dragon reappeared, the beautiful patterns from the stream shimmering over his body, enhancing the majesty of his imposing figure. He gracefully lay down, making sure to keep a respectful distance from her. Obviously, her ploy to hide her fear wasn't working. If she could keep him talking that should ensure her survival long enough to plan her getaway.

"You asked me how our relationship was going earlier. I think you've been rather rude. You haven't even told me your name."

She figured she'd leave out the fact that he'd taken her prisoner. *The word "rude" doesn't really cover kidnapping.* Her snide thought made her lips curve up in a brief smile despite herself.

"Ha!" His laugh was deep and sonorous, and it made her feel safe, for a moment. "Fair point. They call me Arius. Son of Talegar and Valenta." He lowered his head in a slight bow, but a small smile pulled the edge of his mouth up, betraying his amusement at her remonstration. "Please accept my sincere apologies for my lack of manners. I should have introduced myself earlier. Please, tell me about yourself."

"I'm Seraphina Azura. As I told you earlier, I'm a Tracker for the MRO. I live in an apartment in Mandar City. My father, Allen, is also a Tracker."

"And your mother?"

She winced as she said the next sentence. "My mother, Elisabeth, died when I was young." Tears pricked the back of her eyes and she pinched the bridge of her nose to force them back.

Why, in the name of the Four Gods, am I crying? I haven't cried for my mother in years. I'm sure as hell not going to start again now. Especially in front of a dragon. She pushed away her sudden gloominess and put it down to the stress of the last twenty-four hours.

Arius snorted softly and lowered his eyes. "I am sorry." He paused, seeming unsure of what to say. "You must be famished. I shall fetch you some food and water."

As he strode to the back of the cave once more, she couldn't help but reflect on her early years. Her mother had died when she was one, so even as a little girl she sometimes travelled with her father on his less dangerous tracking missions for the MRO. They had no other family in the city, and only an old family friend, Del, could babysit her. This forced her to learn the Tracking trade young, which put her ahead of her peers during her apprenticeship at MINATH. Unfortunately, that put a target on her back, making it difficult to gain friends. This made her graduation a dreaded event.

Upon completion of their apprenticeship, the MINATH students received a ranking from highest to lowest in their respective programmes. The top-scoring Hunter had the first choice of which Tracker they wished to partner with. Sera hadn't expected to be anyone's first choice. She had assumed she would be chosen last by the lowest graded Hunter. As had everyone else. It was a shock to all the Apprentices when she was chosen by Tyler Grayson, the top-performing Hunter of their year and the most popular and influential boy at MINATH. At first, she'd thought it must be a mistake, a joke. But he was deadly serious.

With her twenty-second birthday approaching, she had been a fully-fledged Tracker for a year now and hadn't enjoyed her pairing with Tyler so far. Her father was always telling her about duty, and what an honour it was to be chosen first. But he didn't know what Tyler was really like. None of them did.

Arius brought her a jug of water from the stream along with a glass. She inspected it quizzically.

What need does a dragon have for a glass?

"I hope you don't mind, but I fetched the doe you killed yesterday from your campsite," he said as he pushed the freshly cooked hunk of meat towards her. "I thought it would be a waste of a life if we let her body spoil without being used."

Sera's stomach rumbled and she frowned. "That's fine... but if you found the doe, did you happen to find my backpack?" She crossed her fingers. If he had her backpack she could try to sneak her phone out and call for help.

Arius paused before answering, his steady gaze unnerving her. "No, I didn't."

Disappointment twisted in her gut. There would be no rescue mission by the MRO if they didn't know where to find her.

"What about you?" she asked, dropping her eyes and trying to deflect his piercing look. "I've told you my life story, but you've barely told me anything about yourself."

"Not much to tell, really." He turned away and said, "I hunt, I sleep, I suffer the arrogance of my brother, I abide by my father's law when I must, I enjoy my sister's companionship on the rare occasion we meet without my father's presence, and I avoid your lot." A half-smile quirked the corner of his mouth up, baring his fangs.

Despite his genial tone, she shuddered as she appraised the lethal points. Everything about him exuded a wild strength that frightened her; his body was that of a warrior. His weapons were in the shape of the four horns that swept back from his skull, useful for hooking under an opponent's jaw and piercing their neck. His talons could crush and slice apart any enemy, and those fangs could tear a foe to shreds in seconds. Even his wings had sharp hooks at the joints for slashing into prey. That wasn't even taking into consideration the fact that he could breathe fire. His armour took the form of the lines of spines that flowed from his neck to the tip of his tail, to the hard plates that protected his throat and underbelly. The muscles that rippled underneath the scales that covered his hide cemented the sense of invincibility he wore like a cloak. She tore her gaze away from his body, fear settling into her bones.

There's no way I'm getting out of here alive.

After she had eaten the meat he cooked for her, she stared out of the cave entrance into the empty sky. The sun was setting behind the mountain she was holed up in, the rays splitting into fractured beams of light, smearing the clouds with splashes of colour. Misery clouded her thoughts, hiding the beauty before her, hopelessness sucking away her drive to continue looking for an escape. Depression stole into her mind. Although her mind screamed to keep fighting for freedom, she couldn't find the motivation to pursue it. Throat thick with unshed tears, she lay down, her back to the dragon, closed her eyes and prayed for the sweet release of sleep.

CHAPTER SIX

~THREE WEEKS AGO~

A PAIR OF TITTERS flitted around her head before Sera flicked a hand up to shoo them away. The annoying birds darted away and landed on a digital noticeboard, whispered to one another, peeked back at her before snickering and taking off again. She sighed in good-natured annoyance, knowing there was nothing to be done about the little pests. Her gaze fell on the noticeboard as it flickered with an ad about an inner-city skyrise that had recently been built. The large display proclaimed that they had apartments suitable for humans and mythics alike. It showed photos of a room with a tree trunk in the centre, nests for beds, and open windows that allowed flighted creatures to enter from the air. Another room was for water-based creatures, another for those that preferred the drier climates, along with standard apartments for humans. Sera sighed. It seemed such a shame not to spend their resources on fixing up the old buildings that had been left to fall into decay following the war.

The ad faded and was replaced by the country's Coat of Arms, a large navy "M" surrounded by a triangular pattern fanning behind it like a sunrise with the words "Veritas Vetutis" below. An image of President Kaesus appeared over the top of the Coat of Arms. He had come into power sixty years ago, shortly after the Mythic War, but he didn't look a day over fifty. Dark hair framed his face, with silver strands just showing at his temples. A dark blue suit complemented his intense blue eyes, but no matter how much other women admired his good looks, Sera always felt perturbed when she saw his face. A new regulation appeared beside his picture, reading:

"Regulation # 453: Henceforth, all individuals and community groups proposing public rallies must have completed and submitted Form 713A to the Department of Community Services (DOCS) thirty days prior to the event. The organising committee will not hold any event without receiving formal approval from DOCS. Any committee member or community group not adhering to the above requirement will be subject to incarceration in Iniques Rehabilitation Centre."

Sera's eyebrows raised. *That seems a bit excessive. I wonder if this has come about after Tormund's rally?*

One of her teachers from MINATH, and the only hippogryph on the staff, was always spouting the latest conspiracy theory to his students. Quick to anger but easily distracted, she had always considered him a harmless old mythic. A few weeks ago, he had hosted a small gathering at a park where he claimed that dragons still existed, and the President was hiding the truth from the people of Mandar. Rereading the last sentence of the statement, she shuddered. The Iniques Rehabilitation Centre looked like a high-security prison from the outside, but the Negotiators provided therapy and mediation to the inmates who had committed misdemeanours. Those that had been tried and found guilty of felonies were executed. Cocking her head, she thought about Tormund. She realised she hadn't seen him on his usual flight to work for the last week.

Surely, they wouldn't have detained him at the IRC? This regulation wasn't in effect when he got up on his soapbox.

She shook her head, banishing the thought. He was bound to have gone away on one of his frequent expeditions into the wilderness to search for lost relics.

Another ad slid onto the screen, this time a collection of wanted notices from local shops. A jeweller was offering a decent price for gold, a local workshop was looking for welding apprentices, and one of the stallholders from the Mandar City Market was chasing animal hides. Sera fingered the blade that always hung at her side and gazed thoughtfully into the distance. She enjoyed hiking and camping on her weekends off, and she desperately needed a break from Tyler.

As if her thoughts had summoned him, Tyler stepped out of a gunsmith shop across the street. Sera's heart rate increased as she quickly sought cover. With no other options, she stepped behind the noticeboard and prayed to Ghaia he hadn't seen her. She didn't dare peek out in case the movement caught his eye. Having to deal with his grating personality all week was more than enough, she couldn't bear to see him on weekends too. She started as a finger caught a lock of her hair and tucked it back into place behind her ear.

"What's a beautiful and talented Tracker like yourself doing hiding away over here." Tyler's voice crept over her skin, leaving her feeling like oil had stained her core.

"Hunter Tyler," came her stiff reply.

"Come on, Sera, no need to be so formal! You and me, babycakes, we're the best team in the MRO. It's time we were a team outside of work too." He slid a hand over her shoulders with too much familiarity and slipped it possessively down to her hip.

"Don't touch me, Tyler," she spat, stepping out of his grasp.

His grey eyes flashed before he pulled his mask back into place. A friendly smile that failed to reach his eyes put her on edge. He combed his fingers through his sun-kissed hair, styling it carefully before glancing over his shoulder. Sera followed his gaze and realised that the street was empty. A warning shiver raced up her spine. Catching her by surprise, he slammed her body face forward against the noticeboard. The cold bite of a pistol pressed against her back.

"Don't test me, Sera. You would be nothing without me. You owe me. If I hadn't chosen you as my Tracker, you would have been picked last. Your Hunter would have been Vashti. You know she hates you. If you were ever in danger during a mission, she would let you die. You're lucky I chose you."

"Let me go. You're hurting me." She could fight her way out of the position if she wanted, but last time she tried that, he had pulled some strings and gotten her suspended from work without pay for a fortnight.

He pressed himself closer to her, pinning her frame tightly against his, and ran his hands slowly along her body, savouring each curve. He grabbed a fistful of her loose hair and tilted her head toward him. "I can do what I want. I own you."

At the sound of the gunsmith's door opening, he let her go and stepped back. His eyes were stormy as he tugged the front of his jacket closed.

"See you at the office, babycakes." He flashed a smile with a silent promise that things weren't over yet.

She shuddered uncontrollably as he sauntered down the street. She needed a boiling shower to scrub away the darkness he had left on her soul.

CHAPTER SEVEN

OPENING HER EYES AFTER a restless night, Sera lay
still on the floor of her prison. She focused on keeping
her breathing even as she observed her surroundings,
a tactic she had learnt at MINATH to centre herself
and remain composed under pressure. The dawn was
breaking, the sun's warmth seeping into the cave, filling
her with the hope a new day brings. A moth fluttered
nearby and landed on the shadowy side of one of the ribs
in front of her. Drops of water fell from the stalactites
intermittently, splashing onto the rocky floor. Moss hung
in the shadows, untouched by the sunlight. Ants busi-
ly marched in line, engrossed in their own little world,
without a thought for the plight of the trapped woman.
Her eyes darted to the ceiling, having caught a flickering
movement above her head; a beautiful honeyeater flitted
around the cave. Golden plumage covered the bird's little
body with flecks of jade green under its wings. Its back
was a vibrant splash of indigo that she glimpsed as it
flitted away from her towards the mouth of the cave
where it landed on one of Arius' four horns. He sat mo-
tionless at the lip of the cave, staring east, so still he could
have been cast from bronze. The rising sun's light glinted
off his copper scales, emphasising his majesty. With a
gentle shake of his head, he dislodged the honeyeater

and looked toward her cage. The morning glow threw the spines lining his jaw into sharp relief against the pale sky. Captor or not, he was still a fine specimen of a beast.

She was startled out of her reverie with a loud grumble from her stomach cramping, eager for breakfast. The cloud of dejection that seeped into her soul last night had abated, replaced by a renewed sense of purpose. She had to escape, if for no other reason than to return to her father. He wouldn't survive on his own if she died here. He had no one else. Her resolve hardened.

I won't let that happen. I won't give up. I must do everything I can to get back to Dad.

First, she would eat. Then, she would make an escape plan. Determined, she rolled to her feet, her boots clicking against the bony prison. The dragon stood and turned sharply at the sound and stalked toward her.

"You didn't sleep well," he stated, peering down at her through the ribs. Sera felt very small with his massive body looming over hers and glared at his unsolicited proximity.

"You would be correct in your assessment," she snapped back.

Fear, hunger and exhaustion were making her less tolerant than usual, so she pinched the bridge of her nose and inhaled slowly. It wouldn't do any good to anger a dragon, no matter how kind he had been so far. She was still his prisoner.

Arius' brows pulled down, hooding his eyes as his lips curled up over his teeth. "You would do well to remember who is caring for you, Seraphina." A low growl slid from between his jaws. "You will need to watch your tone. I am not the only one troubled by your power. Others may not be so forgiving of your outbursts as I."

Conciliatory now, she ducked her head and apologised. "I'm just so tired. So much has happened in the last two days. It's a lot to take in. I'm sorry if I caused offence."

His expression softened and he snorted softly in her direction. She had expected his breath to reek of raw meat and death, but it didn't. A vision of curling up beside a warm fire on a winter's night after enjoying a hearty meal filled her mind. She shook her head, trying to dispel the feelings of comfort and security he had evoked within her. He was a dragon, and therefore couldn't be trusted.

"You are forgiven. As it is, you can catch up on your rest today. I must take my leave of you now. I'm going hunting. I shall return to you tomorrow." He placed another haunch of meat beside her cage. "I will leave fresh water and more of the venison here, should you wish to eat." He hesitated before continuing, "Do try not to get into trouble while I'm gone."

What? He's worried about me now? Or is that his way of saying, don't try to escape? "I don't think I can cause too much trouble stuck in this cage." She raised an eyebrow at him. "But thanks for your concern."

He snorted. Whether he was annoyed or amused, she couldn't tell. With that, he leapt into the emptiness and gave an almighty beat of his wings; the powerful back-draught buffeted her body and swirled her auburn hair around her face. By the time she had tucked the errant strands back behind her ears, he had disappeared into the clouds.

Her face flushed, her breathing heavy, Sera flopped down onto the floor of her prison. After devouring the meat Arius had left her, the gamey flavour overpowering her tastebuds, she had tried everything she could think of to escape. She had tried to squeeze out between every rib, but all the gaps were too narrow. She had tried to climb every one of the bones of her cage but the moisture from the cave made them too slick for her to gain purchase on. She had shoulder barged every bone until her body was too sore to take any more. Not one had budged. The stalagmites on each end were unnaturally smooth and wide at the base with a tapered point metres above her head, making it impossible to get out that way. After a quick scan around to ensure she was alone, she had even taken her shirt and trousers off and tied them together to make a cloth rope. After tossing her makeshift rope toward the tips of the ribs above her head until her shoulders ached, she had to concede it wasn't long enough. She'd been attempting to escape for hours with no sign of progress.

I wish I had Firinne.

It might have helped her in her escape plans. At the very least, if she had her knife, she would feel slightly more equipped to handle the dragon.

Eyeing the cooked venison, she sat down with a groan. She announced to the empty cave, "I'm going to get bored with only eating meat soon. I wonder if the dragon would accept a request for some greens to be added to the menu?"

She started giggling at her own joke, stupid as it was. The cackling became unhinged and morphed into sobs of hysteria that bounced around the open space. She was no closer to escaping than she had been yesterday. She would die in this cave and her father would never find her. Tears continued to flow down her cheeks as she thought of her only family member. Her heart squeezed in her chest and she sucked in gasps of air. Letting go, she allowed the panic to consume her for a moment. Then, dragging in deep breaths, she focused on relaxing her shoulders. Slowly, she drew the pieces of her sanity back together. She was exhausted and disheartened. She would rest for a time, gather her strength, and try again. Sera made a vow to herself. She would not give up. Eyelids heavy, she allowed her eyes to close and drifted off to sleep.

CHAPTER EIGHT

~TWO WEEKS AGO~

THE RAIN MISTED THROUGH the city's high-rises, washing the grime of the day from Sera's skin. She turned her face up to the sky, enjoying the feel of each drop on her body. Every time she had to work in close quarters with Tyler Grayson, she left feeling like her skin was covered in an oil slick that she couldn't remove without scrubbing it away in a boiling shower. Unfortunately, since he was her assigned Hunter, they were partnered until retirement unless one of them was killed in the field, so there was nothing she could do to escape him.

She flattened herself against a grey building and waited as a tauron trotted past her, trying to keep dry. The half-man, half-bull, was clutching his briefcase to his chest along with a paper filled binder. Waiting and watching were the main parts of her job. She would find clues to the whereabouts of a rogue mythic by speaking with locals, following the target's physical tracks, or by seeking out the remnants of magic that they often left behind. Back at MINATH the students sometimes joked that Trackers needed their own type of magic to find the beasts. It was just a joke though, everyone knew that only the mythics had access to magic. Studying this particular tauron, she noted the glasses that kept sliding down his nose, the ink-stained hands and the logo of the Mandar City Bank branded on his hindquarters.

A banker through and through.

Recalling her studies, she contemplated their world's history. She was so used to the way things were, she couldn't imagine what it was like before the Peace Covenant. Centuries ago, the magical beasts that roamed the land were thought to be fiction, a lie made up by parents to scare children into behaving themselves. Two hundred years ago, the world had entered a golden era of abundance and peace, at which time the population of mythical creatures had expanded and shown themselves to the humans. In an effort to keep the peace, the government had formed the Mandar Institute for Negotiators, Alchemists, Trackers and Hunters along with the Mythic Relations Office. Their purpose was to foster positive relations between the human race and the creatures that had previously been thought of as fables. For a little over a century the inhabitants of both the human and mythic races worked together to create a new world where they worked side by side.

As she continued walking home, she noticed the bustle of the city seemed more frantic than usual as humans and creatures alike hurried to get out of the rain. Sera kept her pace steady and relished the change in the temperature as the humidity seeped away. Unbidden, her feet stopped in front of a shop. Peering through the display window, she smiled as she saw the gargoyle, Alistair, busy making a new stone carving. She always loved stopping in to see his latest creations. He glanced up from his work, bared his teeth in his awkward version of a grin and beckoned her in. The tinkle of the bell as she entered was welcoming and familiar, and she took a moment to admire the life-size carving of a hippogryph that took up most of the front room.

"Seraphina." Alistair slowly nodded his heavy head in greeting.

"Hey, Alistair. You know I keep telling you to call me Sera."

The gargoyle shrugged a shoulder and returned his attention to his current piece of art. He didn't speak much, but when he did she made sure she listened. The sound of his diamond-tipped fingernails carving into the piece of stone grated on her ears, but it was worth it to see the creation he revealed with each pass of his hands.

He inclined his head toward the stone hippogryph in front of her and grunted, "Tormund modelled for me."

She whistled. "It's just beautiful. As your art always is. Although, I do sympathise for your poor ears if Tormund was your model." She giggled. Her old teacher was notorious for talking the ear off anyone who stayed still long enough. Coupled with the mostly silent Alistair, it painted an amusing scene.

"I guess you haven't had much time for any other new pieces if you've been busy sculpting the hippogriff?"

"Not much." His voice scraped like sand against stone. He paused for a moment as if debating whether to tell her. "There is one new piece."

"May I see it?" she asked, always eager to admire his handiwork.

He jerked his granite wing toward the back corner of his shop, behind the counter. A myriad of small carvings, no larger than the size of her hand, cluttered the low shelf. She had seen them all before. Her brows knitted together as she carefully moved some aside and found the newest addition. She gasped and quickly dropped her hand away. Eyes wide, she turned back to Alistair. He sat as still as any of his sculptures, his back turned to her.

"You made a *dragon*?" she hissed quietly. "Alistair! You have to hide this. If you get reported…" She ran her hands through her hair anxiously. "You know it's not allowed."

He turned to face her and stated, "It's for you."

"For me?" she squeaked. "You know I've always wanted one of your artworks, but I can't accept this. If the MRO finds out about it, you will end up in the IRC and I would, at the very least, get fired. There is no tolerance when it comes to the discussion of dragons." She whispered the last sentence, afraid someone on the street might overhear them.

"I won't tell if you won't."

Exasperated, she rolled her eye. "Of course I won't tell on you."

"Do me a favour then. Pick it up. Look at it. And leave it here. I'll keep it safe for you."

Worry consumed her, making her feel sick. "I'm scared," she said softly.

"Will you live your whole life by other people's rules?" His pupils bored into her.

"This is the law, not a simple matter of deciding whether to ignore the fashion police and wear socks with sandals," she muttered. Sighing, she buried her fear. "Fine. I'll have a look at it, and then walk away and pretend I never saw it."

Gritting her teeth, she forced herself to ignore her training and turned back to the shelf. Gingerly, she picked up the miniature dragon and cradled it in the palm of her hand. Running her eyes over the extinct mythic, she couldn't help but admire every facet of the creature that Alistair had painstakingly carved. The exquisite detail of the scales that covered its body almost made it look like it was writhing in her grasp. The wings were flared wide, and somehow Alistair had made them appear almost translucent. Each tiny claw, tooth and spine was accounted for. But what captured and held Sera's attention were the small sapphires that glinted in the eyes. Enraptured, she ran her fingers along the snout and stroked the precious stones. They flared like blue fire and an electric thrill swept through her veins. She cried out in shock and quickly shoved it back on the shelf.

Glaring at Alistair accusingly, she asked, "Did you know that would happen?"

"That what would happen?" he responded innocently.

Maybe I imagined it. Maybe it was just a trick of the light. She struggled to give herself a logical explanation.

"Never mind." She shivered, the blue orbs still burning in her mind's eye. "I have to get home, Alistair. I'll try to visit again next week." Hugging her arms around her torso, she hurried out of his shop and back into the pouring rain.

CHAPTER NINE

AS SHE SLEPT, DREAMLIKE images filtered through her mind like a sieve. She couldn't quite grasp any of the fleeting visions that ran like water through her hands. A blast of energy encompassed her body as she was propelled forward into Arius' consciousness once more. She could hear the wind whistling over his wings, feel the chill of the night air as tiny frost crystals gathered along his wingtips. Sera felt the strain in his muscles as Arius flapped his wings hard, shaking the ice from his limbs and pushing the air away from him as he came in to land on an exposed mountaintop. A storm crackled around him, lightning sparking briefly before vanishing and stealing the light away with it. The bright flashes followed by such darkness made it challenging to make out their surroundings. Suddenly, three dragons emerged from the cloud-filled sky. One was an opalescent white, delicate and feminine as if birthed by Caelhi, the Goddess of Air. The next, even larger than Arius and shining gold, was surely a son of Bhelanos, the God of Fire. The last was darker than the night that surrounded them, an inky pool of pure muscle. His malevolent presence was more demon than god-like. They joined Arius in the clearing on the mountain. The beating of their wings combined to create their own thunder. As they landed, the storm calmed and a quiet settled over the evening. The dragon that shone like an opal walked towards Arius and gently nuzzled under his chin.

"Little brother, you look well." Her voice was full of pride and her eyes shone with affection for Arius.

Arius nuzzled her back. "It is good to see you too, sister." He blew a gentle puff of smoke towards her.

"Son." A crisp nod from the second dragon was all the notice he was given as his father folded his golden wings tightly into his body.

Arius nodded curtly back.

The black dragon seemed to materialise out of the gloom, his colour blending with the night. He snaked his head forward, his teeth bared in a menacing grin. "Hello, little brother."

"Desamor, it is good to see you." It seemed to Sera that Arius was hiding a layer of sarcasm in his greeting.

Desamor snorted. "Just as it is good to see you, I am sure."

She shuddered. This creature was more like the type of dragon she had expected when she first met Arius. His thinly veiled aggression made her skin crawl.

Would you please stop it? Your fear is very distracting. Arius' voice rang in her mind, but no sound came from his mouth.

Sera started at the unexpected contact before scrambling to exit from his consciousness, but only succeeded in tangling herself up further. She continued to struggle to extract her mind from his but couldn't find the way out.

Just be quiet and don't do... whatever it is that you're doing.

She stilled and tried to make herself into a small ball in the back of his mind, so as not to disturb him.

"Arius, my dear one, you seem far away. Are you all right?" His sister cocked her head as she scrutinised him.

"There had better be a good reason you have broken the terms of your banishment, Arius." The golden dragon's voice was severe as he peered down his snout in disdain.

"Thank you for your concern, Aliah, I am fine, but I have come seeking guidance." Arius paused and began pacing, trying to explain the situation clearly. "I requested this meeting with all of you to discuss an issue that has me confused as to what the right course of action is. I was hunting near the Mandar Ranges two nights past when I sensed a foreign mind enter my own."

The three dragons shifted uneasily at his words, and his sister asked, "What were you doing so far east?"

"I normally don't fly so close to that Goddess-forsaken city, but I was following up on a tip from a Lynx. When I felt my mental defences had been breached, I followed the magic trail and came across a human woman. She appears to have no knowledge of what she did or how she did it. She did not attack me or try to take control, but I don't understand how she entered my mind without force. I have taken her captive and am holding her in my cave at present. Before I decide on whether to allow her to return home, I would ask your opinions on the matter."

Talegar eyed Arius almost lazily as he used a talon to pick at his teeth. "You don't think your ability to shield your mind has simply become weak over the years of your exile?"

A quiet growl rumbled from Arius' chest at his father's jibe. "No. I am as strong as I ever was, both in body and mi—" An invisible force smashed into his consciousness, cutting him off mid-sentence. He bared his fangs and threw up his defences. Sera huddled low behind the wall he had created in his mind to stop the attack. As quickly as it had begun, the attack stopped.

"I see you tell the truth." Talegar flared his wings slightly, seeming annoyed at not being able to gain access into his son's mind.

Desamor spoke then. "If his mind isn't weak, and the human gained access as he claims, then she poses a distinct threat to our kind. We must protect ourselves and remove the danger."

Aliah interrupted him. "Brother, we cannot decide here and now on the woman's fate. We must speak with her."

"But if she has access to his thoughts, who is to say she doesn't have access to his secrets... our secrets! We have no time to lose! We must attack now!" Desamor growled, his tail whipping from side to side in agitation.

Arius snarled at his brother. "She deserves a fair trial at the very least!"

Talegar watched his children bicker between themselves for a few moments more before loosing a deep-throated roar. "Enough. Arius, you will keep the human contained for the time being. See what you can learn of her abilities over the next few days. We three will travel to you and meet her following the setting of the next full moon. We will ascertain the truth, observe her abilities and pass judgement. If you deign to ignore my instructions, you will suffer the consequences. And I swear to Caelhi, if you choose not to heed my command, I will make you miss your days in exile."

Without waiting for a response, Talegar leapt from the mountaintop and disappeared into the storm. Aliah cast a sad glance back at Arius before she too took off. Desamor crouched in preparation to leap into the sky but first flung a contemptuous scowl towards his younger brother. His piercing eyes shone with a deep-seated hatred that left Sera reeling. She felt herself being sucked backwards, out of Arius' mind and back into her regular dreams.

CHAPTER TEN

A PECULIAR CHITTERING SOUND roused Sera from her slumber. Opening her eyes, she observed the pink light of dawn dust the world in a rosy hue. Glancing through her prison bars towards the back of the cavern, she noted that Arius hadn't returned from his hunt yet. The cave echoed with the noise again. Somewhere between giggling and shrieking; she recognised the call of a night scamp. The noise amplified as more night scamps joined in. She looked up to find the vicious little creatures crawling down the wall of the cave towards her. The claws on the end of their leathery wings dug into the rock as their round, voluminous eyes fixated on her. Their disproportionately large ears constantly swivelled, ensuring they were rarely surprised by would-be attackers. The night scamps were only small, but they travelled and hunted in large colonies of a hundred or more. This meant that, even though their sharp, needle-like teeth were tiny, when the colony attacked they could strip the flesh off their prey in minutes.

Sera remembered her training on night scamps well; the best way to deal with them before they attacked was to blow a high-pitched whistle. Their massive ears kept them safe from predators but were also a weakness to be exploited as they couldn't stand any shrill noise. All

Trackers and Hunters were equipped with a whistle as part of their standard survival kit. Unfortunately, it was still in her backpack at her campsite. She knew from her studies that the next best thing was fire. The bonfire Arius had lit before leaving was dwindling as it devoured the last of the logs. In any event, she couldn't reach it from her cage. So, there was no hope of help there either. She frantically flicked her eyes around, hunting for anything she could use as a weapon. Her eyes fell on the heavy metal water pitcher Arius had left with her. Very slowly, she edged towards it, careful not to make any sudden moves. She wrapped her fingers around the handle and, ever so cautiously, rose to her feet, never taking her eyes off the night scamps. The closest one was only a few metres away from her now, with the rest of the colony close behind it. Their chittering rose into a crescendo before abruptly going silent. They had all stopped deathly still, and a hundred pairs of eyeballs glowered at her. All that Sera could hear now was her panicked breathing and her racing heartbeat pounding in her ears. She tightened her grasp on the pitcher, ready to swing it when they attacked, knowing it was futile. One blunt weapon was no match for thousands of savage little fangs.

In the blink of an eye, the colony launched as one and flew down to attack her. The night scamps had to break formation to manoeuvre through the rib cage that surrounded her, giving her a chance to fight them in a more disjointed group than she would have if she were out in the open. Wildly swinging her makeshift weapon, the heavy jug connected with several little bodies. Their lifeless forms fell broken to the floor, causing their comrades to shriek in anguish. She screamed as she swung her arm, praying that her piercing yell would affect their hearing as well. They continued their violent assault on her and the skin on her forearm started to tear. A wild little scamp had clamped down on her arm and hung on desperately as she tried to shake him off. Unable to dislodge the creature, she dashed her arm against the closest rib, killing the creature instantly. His teeth were buried so deeply in her flesh that he stayed lodged in place, fierce even in death. More night scamps fell to her heavy blows with the jug, but many more were there to take their place. She could feel the cruel slice of their sharp teeth all over her body and knew it wouldn't be long now before they found an artery. She would be damned if she gave up without a fight though, a mantra her father had instilled in her from a young age.

She directed all her energy to taking out as many of the scamps as she could, her world shrinking to the small bubble of chaos around her, so it was a great surprise when a stream of fire blazed above her head. Charred frames fell out of the air, while the rest of the scamps screeched and attempted to fly away. Another jet of flames destroyed any hope of escape for them. Sera looked around in a daze, still clutching her pitcher, and saw him; Arius, in all his glory, wings fanned open in aggression, fire spewing from his maw, with the sun rising behind him. She had been so sure death was near that she nearly collapsed from relief. Reaching out a taloned hand, he deftly scooped her out of the ribcage and placed her softly down beside the stream.

Worry clouded his features as he asked, "How serious are your injuries?"

As the adrenaline of the fight began to wear off, Sera assessed the damage to her body. "It hurts, but it's not life-threatening."

Baring her teeth in a silent snarl, she began working the scamp's small body back and forth, slowly prising its fangs from her arm. She cringed as she felt its fragile bones snap under the pressure from her fingers. Throwing its crushed body away, she winced as she lowered herself into the stream and began gently washing her injuries. Gritting her teeth, she hissed in pain as the water washed over her wounds. She knew she had to clean them if she was to avoid any of them getting infected. It was hard to watch as her shredded skin wafted in the stream.

"Are you all right?" Apprehension rolled off him in waves, but she wasn't in the mood to deal with his unwelcome concern.

"I'm pissed off, actually." She glared at him. "I nearly died from a simple night scamp attack because I didn't have any way to protect myself or anywhere to hide. It's your fault that I am so helpless I could have been taken out by those little bastards. I need my knife. I need my rifle." She groaned as the pain obscured her ability to check her words. "I need my old life back! It wasn't anything special, but it was mine. I at least had some semblance of control. I wish I had never decided to go camping. I wish I had never met you! You ruined everything." Tears leaked from her eyes and she fiercely dashed them away, frustrated to show weakness in front of a dragon.

"Are you quite done?" Arius' voice was an icy rumble, threatening to consume her like a winter's storm, the earlier concern for her wellbeing expired.

She turned away from him and refused to answer, petty as the action might be, as the blood seeped out of her torn flesh.

Arius snaked his head forward until his right eye hovered directly in front of her face. "The way I see it," he mused, "is that you should be thanking me."

"Thanking you!" Sera exclaimed and tried to leap up, but the pain in her body prevented her. With a splash, she thumped back into the stream and wiped her tear-stained cheeks. "Why in the name of Ghaia should I be thanking you?"

"Well, I did save your life," came the smug response.

Sera opened her mouth to argue and closed it again. She frowned sullenly as the slitted pupil in the emerald iris filled her vision. "Technically, yes. You did save my life. But I wouldn't have needed saving if you had left my weapons with me. Or better yet, if you had left me alone in the first place."

Arius turned his head so he faced her. "I will apologise for taking you against your will. However, I still stand by the fact that I believed you were a threat. Try to see it from my point of view. If you were Tracking a mythic and stumbled across someone acting abnormally, would you not report it to your Hunter?"

Sera sighed begrudgingly. *He has a point, I suppose.*

CHAPTER ELEVEN

ARIUS MOVED HIS SNOUT forward and gently pressed it against her chest. She gasped at his touch. A low hum rumbled in his throat as he closed his eyes and froze in that position. Sera marvelled at his great head, her injuries momentarily forgotten. The power he exuded was almost overwhelming. The copper scales covering his jaws shone in the morning light as if lit from within. Reaching up, she placed her hands on his skin. The warmth that flooded her from the contact made her heart pound and her breath hitch. It was a surreal moment in time, one that she could have never imagined, even in her wildest dreams. How could she regret meeting him? She caressed his cheek, running her hands over him, awestruck by his magnificence. He exhaled softly and opened his eyes, contemplating her for a moment more before withdrawing. The loss of their physical connection hit Sera like a brick wall, and she tried to hide her face as tears spilled unbidden onto her cheeks once more.

This isn't right. I am not upset about him pulling away. My cuts hurt, that's all it is. The pain worsened as she returned her attention to the lacerations covering her body. Keeping her eyes lowered, Sera murmured, "Thank you, Arius. If you hadn't arrived when you did, I don't think I..." she shivered, unable to finish the sentence, knowing how close to death she had come. "I'm... sorry. That I lashed out. I don't regret meeting you."

"I too am relieved I made it back in time," he murmured, eyeing her tattered flesh.

"If only I had my backpack," she cringed again from the pain, "I have a poultice in it that would accelerate the healing process and halt any infection."

At that, Arius briskly turned away from her and padded quickly past the large boulder that hid the mysterious opening. When he reappeared, something brown and bulky hung from his mouth by straps.

"My backpack!" Sera exclaimed. She glared at him. "You lied to me! I thought you said you didn't find it?"

Dropping the backpack on the floor, Arius shuffled his feet sheepishly. "Well... technically, I did not lie. It was not I who found it. A friend of mine did, and he gave it to me. Therefore, not a lie. I simply decided not to tell you the whole truth. The important thing is that you have it now."

She frowned at him sternly, then dropped her shoulders in defeat, unable to hold onto her anger any longer. He had saved her life, after all. She grimaced as she struggled out of the stream and shuffled over to the bag and quickly pawed through the contents. Finding the white container of Heal, she liberally applied the cream to the lacerations on her legs, arms, neck and torso. She sighed in relief as the healing balm took effect. It should only take a day or two for the cuts to mend now, with little chance of infection.

"That is intriguing," said Arius. "I can see your poultice is already mending your wounds. Is that not magic?"

"No, but I can understand why you would think so. Our alchemists' abilities are very impressive. We don't have magic, so we utilise technology and science to keep the balance of power even between mythics and humans. Our alchemists develop weapons and medicine that allow us to complete our missions with minimal loss of life on either side."

A nasty little voice inside her wondered if she was giving away too much information to a mythic that she hadn't known still existed until a few days ago.

The path to peace lies in trust. There will never be true peace if one of us doesn't take the first step.

"Fascinating," he said then paused, as if contemplating whether to tell her a secret. "I imagine I must have given you quite a fright." The tip of his tail twitched, and he sighed before continuing, "In truth, you have frightened me. When I sensed your presence in my mind that first night, I had no idea who, or what you were. That has never happened to me before. I pride myself on my ability to shield my thoughts from any creature who attempts to broach my mental defences. And you..." he looked at her with a troubled gaze, "you were just there. There was no attack, no hint of you attempting to enter, when without warning you could see what I saw, feel what I felt. I could feel you with me but I was helpless to stop you. You have great power and you don't even know of it. Which worries me even more. What could happen with your power unchecked and untrained? Having gotten to know you a little more, you don't seem particularly threatening. However, if another human were to discover your talent, they may try to manipulate you, and then all of dragonkind would be at risk." He scrutinised her for a moment. "It may not be limited to dragons either. All of the mythics could be in danger if you were to take advantage, or be taken advantage of by the wrong human."

She raised an eyebrow at him. "Why are we limiting the danger of my manipulation to humans? If you think I have such great power over the mythical world, which, side note, I don't think is the case, couldn't a dragon take control of me?"

Arius' tail flicked like a whip as he rounded on her. "How dare you suggest that? No dragon would ever stoop so low. We are not a lesser class of intelligence who are obsessed with selfish goals of controlling the world."

Her cheeks flushed with fury at his insinuation. "Really? How dare I? How about how dare you? To suggest that humans are a lower form of intelligent life whose only goal is to take over the world. I can't believe you."

She stormed away from him, towards the mouth of the cave. Standing legs apart, arms folded, she stared unseeing into the clear sky. She breathed deeply, trying to calm herself. A little voice in her head reminded her of Tyler's past actions.

Technically, when it came to Tyler, Sera knew that Arius' suggestion of danger was a real threat. He could manipulate any situation to work in his favour. Whether that was bribing an MRO employee to look the other way, or by using his well-known family name to sway the thoughts of a government official to be in line with his desires, Tyler knew how to influence others. She just didn't want Arius to think the worst of the human race as a whole.

There are some bad apples to be sure, but we aren't all rotten.

Out of the corner of her eye, Sera watched Arius approach her slowly. He kept his great head low and unthreatening, staying level with her eyeline.

"I am sorry if I upset you. I should have been more diplomatic with my words." He gently nudged her with his snout in a conciliatory manner.

His touch melted her stiff stance and she sighed. "I shouldn't have reacted the way I did. I will admit that there are a few people I know who would be a danger to the mythic world with too much power. You just act so damn superior. It's frustrating." She rolled her eyes at him.

He chuckled. "One of my many gifts."

"I just don't like you painting us all with the same brush. I know the majority of my colleagues would never use any of my so-called powers to take control of the mythical creatures we share this world with," she grumbled.

Arius' breath tickled her neck. "Well, as you say, it's a good thing you do not have any great powers then."

She frowned, confused by his backtracking and scrutinised him. "Are you making a joke?" she asked incredulously. His chortle answered her question. "I didn't think dragons made jokes."

She joined in with his laughter and tried to shove his head away, as she would to any friend who made fun of her. His head was like a rock, unmoving and massive. She left her hands on his cheek and caressed the bronze scales there, enchanted. Running her fingers over the rough bumps, she noted the odd patterns and many shades of copper and bronze that covered his skin. A warmth tingled through her fingertips, up her arms and down her torso, coming to rest somewhere in her lower abdomen. She gasped and stepped back, breaking contact. This was not a feeling she had ever experienced with anyone else. This was different. Heat coloured her cheeks as she took a few more steps back, hoping the distance would banish the unfamiliar feeling.

He cocked his head, contemplating her retreat. "Are you still afraid of me?"

"No!" she exclaimed, too quickly. Determined not to show any more weakness than she already had, she lifted her chin and looked him in the eye. "I'm not afraid of you."

"You can't lie to me." He smiled. "I am particularly good at seeing through lies, if I do say so myself."

"I'm telling you, I'm not afraid of you!"

He swivelled his head to stare her down. "Hmmm. No. You are not afraid of me. But you are afraid of something. What is it?"

The intensity of his gaze was unsettling and did nothing to eliminate the feelings that smouldered inside her. There was no way she was telling him she was afraid of her budding feelings towards him.

"Don't worry about it," she snapped.

He bowed his head. "I will respect your wishes." He paused before saying, "If there is anything I can do to help, please don't hesitate to ask. If it is within my power I will grant your wish."

"Why do you have to be so damned nice?" she griped under her breath. Aloud, she asked, "I suppose asking to be returned to my home would be too much to ask?" She had to get out of here before these emotions grew unruly and destroyed her will to return to her old life.

Arius blew out a thin spiral of smoke. "I am truly sorry, but I cannot grant you that. Not yet anyway. We need to learn more about your powers and whether you are a threat to our way of life before you can go home."

"And how are we supposed to do that?" she challenged him.

He ducked his head sheepishly, and mumbled, "I have called for the assistance of a Council of dragons to discuss and test your abilities."

"So, that wasn't a dream?" she asked. The scene from last night seemed like it had happened a lifetime ago and she wasn't sure if it was real. The details of the conversation were hazy, and every time she tried to grab hold of the memory it slipped away.

"I'm afraid not. Once you have been assessed we will decide on our next course of action."

"Next course of action? What the hell does that mean?" She nearly shouted the words at him as her fear bubbled up.

"We will decide if you are allowed to return home, or..." he looked away.

Her blood ran cold. *I've got a bad feeling about this.* "Or what, Arius?" she asked quietly.

"If the Council believes that you pose a significant threat with no ability to learn to control your powers, then they may choose to..." he exhaled heavily, "to execute you."

"No." The word escaped her mouth in a sharp exhale as despair flooded her body and she sank to her knees. "So then, this Council of wise dragons that are coming to decide my fate, would you care to tell me how long I have to learn control of a power I never knew I had?" she asked.

"They will be here at first light on the day after the full moon."

She stared at Arius in horror. "That's only four days away! Why did you have to take me away from my camp?" She buried her face in her hands.

"I am sorry, Seraphina. Truly." His voice was hoarse. "If I had known that I..." He shook his wings out. "It doesn't matter now, I did what I did believing it to be the right thing at the time. All we can do is work together to face this challenge head-on and ensure that they don't vote for execution."

"Ha!" Her laugh was one of desperation. "That's just great. And how exactly are we going to do that?"

Arius extended a claw out and, more gently than she thought was possible, moved her hands away from her face. He stared deep into her eyes and said, "We make sure you learn control."

CHAPTER TWELVE

~ONE WEEK AGO~

HER FATHER STRODE CONFIDENTLY ahead of Sera along the rarely used trail. They both carried heavy packs filled with groceries and small goods. This was a secret monthly ritual they had shared since she was a little girl. Pushing aside the bracken that had attempted to over-take the track, they trudged towards the witch's house. She wasn't really a witch, but everyone liked to gossip about the old hermit in the woods. As they approached the timber cabin, Sera could understand why people called Del a spellcaster. Strings of herbs hung from the wall of the hut, pendants made of bones jingled in the light breeze and a stuffed raven perched on the rickety gate. Its beady black eye seemed to stare at them as they approached, and not for the first time, Sera shuddered and quickened her pace past the dead bird. A wizened figure was bent over in the garden, pulling weeds. Del had attempted to tame her grey hair by pulling it back into a braid, but the muggy air had teased it into a flyaway mess. Straightening, she waved and hobbled up to the house to greet them.

"Come in, come in." She shooed them in the door.

"How are you, Del?" Allen smiled jovially as they slung their packs off.

"Fine, fine. Can't complain, no one listens anyway," she grumped.

He winked at Sera and put an arm around the old woman. "You should come and visit us sometimes if you're wanting company."

Shaking her head vehemently, she said, "Nope. I'm never going back into that accursed city. I will live and die in this cabin. You're just putting yourself on the fast track to an early death if you stay in that place." She bit her lip and her eyes slid to Sera's before darting away.

Sera frowned, bewildered. Del often said odd things, but that was a little more pointed than usual.

She limped away quickly and put the kettle on to boil. "Cuppa tea, anyone? I made a cake."

Her father chuckled and perched on the edge of her old wooden table. "That would be wonderful, thank you! But before we settle in, we'll get your groceries unpacked. Come on, Sera."

Allen took his pack to the pantry and started unloading the tinned food as he chatted to Del. Sera swung her bag onto her back and made her way outside to open the hatch to the underground cellar. She carefully descended the dozen steps into the earth and found the candle and matches. She struck the match and watched its flame chase away the shadows that clung to the walls. The damp earthy smell pervaded the air in the small room. With the candle lit, she walked over to the icebox and hefted the lid open.

It's crazy how she lives off the grid like this. I don't know if I could do it.

She began packing the cold food from her pack into the icy chamber. Fingers aching from the cool, she moved quickly, eager to return to the heat of the day. In her haste, she bumped an old cupboard with her shoulder.

Something clattered down from the top, making her wince at the tinkle of broken glass. Getting down onto her hands and knees, she squinted into the darkness. A small photo frame had fallen and smashed apart.

"Shit," she muttered quietly. Fumbling blindly under the cupboard, she caught the edge of the frame with her fingertips and dragged it out. Bringing the candle closer, she gasped when it illuminated the two smiling figures in the photo. It was Del. With Elisabeth.

Her hands shook as she absorbed the image. Del was a few decades older than her mother, but they had their arms draped around each other's shoulders like the best of friends. Hands shaking, she smoothed her thumb gently over her mother's face. They had a few photos of her at her father's house, but she'd never seen this one.

"Are you all right, Sera?"

She dropped the picture in fright and spun around to face the voice, her hand automatically grasping Firinne. Del watched her impassively, the flickering candlelight deepening the wrinkles on her face.

"You… you knew my mother?"

Lips pinching into a grimace, she replied, "Yes." She squeezed her eyes shut. "I knew Eli better than anyone else ever did."

"But… how? How did you know her? And why haven't you spoken of her before?"

Turning away sharply, she shuffled towards the stairs. "Never you mind."

Suddenly angry, Sera threw herself in front of the old woman, blocking her exit and thrusting the candle between their faces. "I was one when she died. I have no real memories of her. Please. You have to tell me."

Del studied her for a moment in silence. Sera felt stripped bare, as if her soul was being measured carefully before being accepted. Making her decision, Del lifted a hand to her throat and raised a locket that had been hidden under her collar. Releasing the latch, she opened it to reveal a lock of auburn hair next to a photo of a baby girl. The little girl's eyes were the same deep blue as Del's were. The old woman wore an expression that spoke of a loss too deep for words. Slowly, Sera began to put the pieces together.

"Was she... was she your daughter?" she whispered. The look the old woman gave her was confirmation enough. She choked out, "But that means—" She shook her head as a strange buzzing sounded between her ears. "That means I'm your granddaughter."

Unable to hold herself upright any longer, she sank onto the bottom step. Her vision swam as she held her head between her hands, desperately trying to keep herself together.

A tangle of questions and thoughts swirled through her mind but the only one she managed to vocalise was, "Why?"

Releasing her breath in a huff, Del sat down on the step beside Sera and rubbed her back. Somehow, the old woman seemed to have shrunk in the last minute.

"I'm sorrier than I can say, Seraphina. I was forbidden from telling you. It was your mother's last wish, to keep you safe. I am still bound by my oath and cannot tell you anything more, for fear of risking your life. If you discover the truth on your own, I will be released from my promise. For now, what I can tell you is that your mother loved you very much. She would be so very proud of the young woman you have become. For that matter, so am I."

She turned into her grandmother's embrace and wept. Through the tears, she stammered out, "I just wish I had known her."

Rocking her slowly, she hummed soothingly. "She would have loved to know you too, pet."

Dazed by the revelation, it took some time before she managed to get a hold of her emotions. Her grandmother stayed by her side and continued to offer her comfort.

Summoning a watery smile, Sera asked her, "So, what should I call you then?"

Stroking the tears from her cheeks with her fingertips, her papery skin as soft as a petal, Del beamed. "Nanna will suit just fine."

CHAPTER THIRTEEN

SITTING UP ON HIS haunches, Arius tilted his head and regarded her quizzically. "After this morning's frightening incident, I think we both need to blow off some steam. Would you like to fly with me?"

Sera's jaw dropped. "Are you being serious?" she squeaked.

He chuckled. "Of course."

Eyes wide and shining, she said, "Yes. Please." He folded his front legs and sank to the ground beside her. He still seemed impossibly tall. "Promise you won't let me fall?" she asked, only half-joking as she clambered up the proffered foreleg.

The bumpy scales made it easy to find handholds before she stretched up and grasped one of the spikes adorning the back of his neck and pulled herself up. A narrow gap in the spines at the base of his neck made an ideal place for her to sit. She swung her legs around the sides of his neck, but her heels didn't even reach halfway. Sera peered down at the cave floor and gulped. Arius stood up, causing her to lurch backwards. She bit back a squeak of fright and grabbed hold of the closest spine.

He spread his wings in preparation for flight and turned his head to look at her. "Are you ready?"

Heart hammering, she grinned. Trying to hide her nerves, she feigned nonchalance and announced loudly, "Sure am."

He bared his teeth in a terrifying grin and loosed a joyful roar into the dizzying drop in front of them. Tucking his wings close to his body, he leapt into the emptiness. There was a moment of suspension before they started to drop like a stone. Sera screamed. The great wings snapped open and filled with air, halting their descent. Arius hung mid-air, floating on an updraft of wind.

All was silent aside from the quiet rush of the waterfall streaming down the mountainside behind them. With a few powerful thrusts from his wings, Arius drew them upwards, past the cave mouth, through the scattered wisps of cloud, before gliding on the wind's currents, only needing the odd stroke to keep them level. At their back, the mountain still loomed high into the skies, but looking eastward, Sera could see for miles. She gazed in awe at the rich tapestry of colours laid out before them. The lush green of the forest, the dark blue shadows of the gullies, the glinting silver of the streams, and the shadowy purple of faraway hills. Peering into the distance, past the barrenness of the Red Waste, she could just make out a charcoal smudge on the horizon that might have been Mandar City.

The air was cold but the heat produced by the dragon's scales kept her warm. Wrapping her arms around his neck to drink in the warmth, she sighed happily as she drank in the sights below her.

"It's so peaceful."

"It certainly is," Arius replied. "Up here, I am happy. Up here, I can be alone with my thoughts. Or I used to be," he corrected himself. Angling his head so he could see her face, he raised an eyebrow, "Would you like to try to emulate your previous venture into my mind? Albeit, with my permission this time." He smiled, turning his head away again.

"I... I don't know how to," Sera stammered. "What if I can't?"

"Don't think like that. If you've done it once, you can do it again. Technically, you've done it twice now." She could hear the smile in his voice. "Just relax."

"I'll try." Sera let her breath out all at once as she tilted her head up.

Keeping her breathing deep and even, she examined the endless blue of the sky. Without any landmarks to watch, it was impossible to tell how fast they were travelling. She loved the warmth of the sun on her face, the rush of the wind as it whipped through her hair. How different it was this time. Instead of being clutched in a cage of talons, petrified for her life, she was perched upon his wither, just in front of his wings, basking in the sunshine. For the first time in her life, she truly felt free. Raising her arms, she released a jubilant holler that was immediately whipped away into the open sky. The world seemed to shift and a shudder ran through her body.

Hello there. A soft voice brushed against her mind.

She recoiled from the foreign contact.

You did it. Pride coloured the voice.

Sera realised that she had made the transfer into Arius' mind, and it was his inner voice speaking that she could hear.

Can you... hear me? she thought to Arius, unsure if it would work.

Yes, he said. *It appears I can feel you in my mind but can only hear the thoughts you project to me. What can you feel?*

Give me a few moments.

She tried to relax in this alien environment. She imagined herself floating like a leaf on a breeze that wafted through his mind. She settled into this new world she found herself in and noticed a light shining in the centre of his consciousness. She drifted forwards and touched it. A shiver rippled through his body and she felt the sensation of falling. The fall halted and Sera sucked in a sharp breath. Or rather Arius inhaled, and she felt his lungs expand. She could hear the wind that whistled past his ears and see the earth through his eyes. The geography of the surrounding land was brought into sharp focus with colours that were more vibrant than anything she'd ever seen before. She realised she had entered another level in his mind and was one with him. An almost hysterical excitement bubbled up inside them, and delight filled her heart when Arius bellowed a joyous roar into the endless sky.

They looked back as one to see her body still perched on his wither. It appeared unconscious, her head lolling from side to side with each beat of his wings, her eyes rolled back with only the whites visible. It was frightening to be able to see herself from the outside but unable to control her body.

Maybe I should go back to my own mind now.

I think that would be wise.

His brow furrowed nervously as he steadied his flight and waited for her to make the transfer. Turning her focus inwards, she tried to trace her way back to her own consciousness. Searching for the light that had led her into the second level, unease settled around her like a blanket when she couldn't find it.

Do you have any idea how I might get back? The thought of being trapped in his mind haunted her.

How did you exit last time?

I don't know. Last time I left my connection with you I was scared out by Desamor. The first time, I felt your decision to hunt me when you realised I was in your head.

Hmmm. Let me mull over it. In the meantime, try saying 'inner peace' a few times.

Are you being serious? She felt his lips turn up into a smirk. *I'm quietly panicking about being stuck in your head and you're busy cracking jokes. Thanks for the help. If I could roll my eyes, I would.*

I have it! His smug jubilation at solving the mystery was obvious. *Or at least, I have a theory. Both times you exited involuntarily because you were scared for your life. If you can't find a way out alone, I can frighten you back into your body.*

Really? That's your plan. You're going to spook me out of your head. Wow.

I'm not guaranteeing it will work, but if you can't find your way back, I am more than willing to help. The smug tone left her exasperated.

Fine. My way first.

On instinct, she concentrated on the steady beats of his wings. She thought of her own body, of the way each stroke made it sway. She listened to the sound of the air streaming over his body. Concentrating, she imagined the feel of it on her skin. She could almost hear the flap of her jacket in the wind. As the sun beat down on their backs, she basked in its warmth, allowing the heat to soak to her core. With a rush, she felt her mind being sucked away like water that had been released into a drain. Gasping, she opened her own eyes and whooped.

"I did it!" she yelled and pumped a fist into the air. Her arm shook with the drain on her energy. Wobbling, she grabbed the spine in front of her and gripped it tightly. "Ghaia! That was close."

"Are you all right?" Concern laced his words as the dragon turned his massive scaled head to check on her.

"Yeah. Thanks. But... could we please go back now?"

Nodding in assent, Arius banked smoothly and glided back towards the monstrous mountain.

CHAPTER FOURTEEN

HAZEL PACED THE FLOOR of the apartment once again. Moonlight dappled the windowsill that looked over the city, but the peaceful ambience did nothing to ease her worry. Sera was supposed to have returned from her camping trip last night. She had never been twenty-four hours late. Hazel had waited as long as she could bear it; all day she had been opening the door to the hallway at every set of footsteps that went past. She checked her phone once more. No messages, no calls. Even though she knew it was likely to get the same result as before, she tried Sera's number again.

"Hey, you've reached Sera, sorry I missed your—"

Hazel snapped the phone shut and resumed her pacing. She was an Alchemist, she wasn't trained to deal with missing persons. She paused at the home workbench she kept stocked with basic ingredients in case she was struck by the inspiration for a new mix. Cocking her head, she contemplated whether she could use anything to create some sort of tracking elixir. Dismissing the notion as quickly as she had thought it, she pulled her phone out again. She would call the office – they'd know what to do.

"Thank you for calling the after-hours service centre of the Mythic Relations Office. This is Marjorie speaking, how may I help you?" The tired voice didn't sound like they wanted to help anyone.

"Maggie! It's Hazel. I need help and I don't know who to talk to. Sera is missing."

"Hazel... sorry, Hazel, what did you say your last name was?"

"Oh my gosh, Maggie, it's Hazel. The Alchemist. You see me every payday."

"Oh right! Of course. Sorry, Hazel, it's been a long day."

"Did you hear what I said? Sera is missing." Before Maggie could ask, Hazel added, "Seraphina Azura. The Tracker paired with Tyler." Hazel would bet her apartment that Maggie wouldn't need to ask for Tyler's last name. Everyone knew Tyler.

"Oh, yeah, I know Sera. Wait, what do you mean she's missing? Does Tyler know?" Maggie asked.

"She was supposed to return from her camping trip last night, and she's never late, and she's not home yet. Something must have happened to her." An edge of hysteria was creeping into Hazel's voice as she voiced her fears aloud.

"It's okay, Hazel. Take deep breaths. I'm sure Sera is fine. She probably just lost track of time. Or maybe she went to visit family? Have you checked in with Tyler in case he knows where she's gone?"

"You don't understand. She wouldn't do that and not tell me about her plans. We need to take action now! Get a search party organised or something!" Hazel hated how relaxed Maggie seemed to be about her missing friend.

Maggie groaned. "Hazel... are you sure about this? It's an awful lot of paperwork if you're wrong. Couldn't we just wait until tomorrow to see if she gets home overnight?"

Blood boiling, Hazel replied icily, "Don't worry about it. I'll call someone else."

Tapping her fingers in agitation, she contemplated whether to call Tyler or Allen, Sera's father. Whilst both Hazel and Sera detested Tyler, he did have connections to powerful people who could start the search for her sooner rather than later. Then again, Allen was an excellent Tracker and knew Sera better than anyone. He might have more luck finding her on his own. Her decision made, she searched in her phone's contacts for his number.

"Hazel. This is a surprise. What's up?" Allen's voice was warm and familiar, and she relaxed a little. Sera's father would know what to do.

"I'm so sorry to call you so late, sir, but I'm worried. Sera hasn't returned from her camping trip. I tried calling the MRO but they just fobbed me off. It's not like her to be late home. Especially by a whole day. Have you heard from her?"

There was a lengthy pause before Allen quietly cursed. His reply, when it came, was tense. "Thank you for contacting me, Hazel. No, I haven't heard from her since our dinner last week. You're right, it's not like her. I'll make some calls and be in touch soon to let you know the plan."

Hazel opened her mouth to respond, but he'd already hung up.

CHAPTER FIFTEEN

SERA FOUND THE TIME slipping away as she grew accustomed to the dragon's presence. More than that, she was enjoying his company. He had listened to her request and foraged for green plants and fruits for her to eat, so she wasn't restricted to his meat-based diet. He left her backpack with her, and she had surreptitiously checked her mobile to confirm her suspicions that there was no reception here. He hadn't confined her in the cage since the night scamp attack and had given her some old furs to sleep on.

He still slept in front of the boulder at the back of the cave to prevent her from exploring the secret area, but she found she didn't mind. The part of her that had been screaming for her to escape had grown quieter with each passing day, but she still felt a pang of remorse when she thought of her father.

He'll be so worried. I'll just wait for the Council to arrive and explain everything. If they're as reasonable as Arius is, they'll let me go home.

She was more comfortable around Arius now but still watched him in awe, disbelieving that a mythic so magnificent, that was supposed to be extinct, would offer her his friendship.

Even if it is only for a little while longer.

As they sat at the edge of the cave, watching the sun climb high into the sky, Sera queried, "Why does everyone believe dragons died out in the Mythic War?"

Arius stiffened for a moment, then cast her a sideways glance. "Not everyone believes all dragons are dead."

"But most do. That's what I was taught at MINATH. Since the war, it's treason to speak of dragons at all, other than to read the history books. Even in those textbooks, the information on dragons is limited. All I was told was that the war started after the Sapphire Dragon murdered Tracker Borin when Hunter Ajax tried to save him from her spell."

A deep snarl startled her. "That's not what happened."

Refusing to be cowed by his anger, she challenged him. "Enlighten me, then."

He fidgeted beside her as he considered his words carefully. "Your Tracker fell in love with her. With the Sapphire Dragon, as you call her. They knew it would never be accepted by either of their people, so they ran away together. The Hunter found them and killed them both and took his lies back to the MRO. It was the Hunter Ajax's deception that instigated the Mythic War." He paused briefly, his mouth pulling down in grief before continuing, "The dragon community was decimated after the war. We lost more than three-quarters of our population. We made the decision to retreat to Sky Valley to recover before facing the world of men again. But your President knew we weren't extinct. I'm sorry to be the one to tell you this, but it was your government who chose to fan the flames of rumour that we were gone forever."

She sat very still, staring out over the earth, as she pondered his words. Her whole world view was shifting, and it was uncomfortable. She ignored her kneejerk reaction to reject the information he had shared and allowed the new knowledge to wash over her. As she tasted the concept of conspiracy, it settled into her bones, and she knew it to be the truth.

"But why would they do that?"

Arius scrutinised her for a long moment before sighing. "I'm not sure." Standing up swiftly, he gave himself a shake. "Would you care to join me for a swim down below?"

She stood and stretched, turning her head to subtly sniff her underarm, and nearly gagged. She had attempted to wash in the shallow stream in the cave but obviously, it hadn't been enough. "That would be wonderful." She climbed up the offered foreleg, her technique growing surer with each day that passed. A thrill travelled up her body at the chance to fly again and a holler escaped her lips when he propelled them from the cave and into the sky once more.

Arius landed heavily in a clearing at the base of the mountain, causing a wave of dust and leaves to billow out from underneath them. Sera heard the crashing of the waterfall and leapt toward the sound as soon as her feet touched the grass. It was a relief to get out of that cave. She hadn't realised how badly she needed to see new sights and feel some texture other than rock. She splashed straight into the glistening pool and gasped as the cold bite of the mountain water wound around her waist and took her breath away. Sucking in a lungful of air she submerged herself, knowing that was the quickest way to acclimatise her body to the chill.

The freezing water rejuvenated her muscles and made her giddy with the sudden energy rush. Popping back to the surface she admired the cascading waterfall that emerged from their cave's entrance, thousands of feet above their heads.

Since when did I start calling it our cave?

She shook off the confusing feelings she was fighting to control and distracted herself by swimming across the tarn. It was a lot wider than she had realised, but it was such a relief to be active after spending the last four days cooped up in the cave she couldn't help but relish the burning in her muscles.

Giggling, she glanced back to where Arius was standing on the bank, swam closer to him and, grinning impishly, swung her arm into the water and splashed him. Snorting, he reared up on his hind legs and stretched his wings out. Sera's jaw dropped as she took in his draconian body. The sharp talons that could lethally gut an animal or gently cradle her body shone in the sun. She could almost see through the thin membrane that covered his wings, and his coppery scales reflected the light bouncing off the water hole. The four horns adorning his head like a crown gave him an aura of splendour. He truly was magnificent. Never had she ever thought she would see such a glorious creature. Such mythics only appeared in the history books.

All thoughts were swept away as Arius leapt into the air, seeming to hover for a moment over the pool, before crashing into the water. His body disappeared beneath the surface but his entrance sent a wave surging towards Sera. Taking a quick breath she ducked underwater to avoid it. She hung suspended in the clear water as Arius glided underneath her, graceful despite his size. He seemed just as at home in the water as above it. His wings were tucked tight into his sides as he slipped through this new world. The dappled sunlight from above filtered down and danced upon his scales, creating fractured reflections on their surroundings that made this moment in time a magical experience. She wanted to stay and watch his graceful movements but realised all too soon that her body was begging for oxygen.

Breaking the surface, she drank in a lungful of air and floated on her back, staring into the sky. Her brows kissed when she noticed, high above her head, a dark shape flit into the cover of a cloudbank. Almost as if it had hidden when it felt her gaze. She shook her head to dispel the unease that threatened to ruin the beautiful day.

It's probably just an eagle. There's no need to be on high alert all the time. Especially when you have a dragon for a friend. She contemplated Arius. Somehow, against her better judgement, he had become her friend. A tendril of thought from deep within her subconscious slithered up and whispered, *You wish he could be more than just a friend though, don't you?* She clamped down on that thought hard and shoved it down into the depths of her mind. *That's not natural. I don't want him in that way. We are pushing boundaries enough as it is.*

Ripples lapped over her drifting form as the dragon emerged beside her. His emerald eye was level with her head when a cheekiness overtook his countenance and he ducked back underwater. She changed position so she was treading water and ducked her head beneath the surface to see what he was up to. A flurry of bubbles blasted her in the face and she reared back, spluttering, before yelping as Arius surged toward her from below. Somehow, she managed to grasp at a spine on his back without being impaled as he hurtled his body into the air, with her perched precariously on top. He spread his wings but didn't beat them, deliberately allowing his body to twist mid-air and do a slow dive back toward the pool.

As they crashed down, a massive wave swept away from them, splashing on to the rocks. Water cascaded over

Sera but she managed to keep her seat. He gradually drifted back to the surface and swam to the shore. Clambering up the boulder, he leaned his shoulder closer to the ground and held his foreleg out for her to slide down. As soon as she'd dismounted, he shook himself, sending droplets spinning away and wetting her. He gave her a lazy smile before lying down with a grunt. Chuckling, Sera gave her own less impressive version of a shake and lay beside him.

As they sleepily basked together on the rocky outcrop, soaking up the sunshine, Arius mentioned, "There is someone I want you to meet."

Sitting up, Sera cocked her head. "Is it one of those dragons from your meeting yesterday?"

"Gods no, they won't be arriving for a few days yet." He frowned and swept his tail along the boulder in agitation, the scales scraping against the rock. "We had better hope they don't, anyway. No, this is a friend of mine. He's curious about you and I've asked for his assistance."

"When?"

"Tomorrow. A warning: he is quite... friendly. He likes being in one's personal space." Arius huffed a smoke ring at some remembered annoyance.

Sera paled. "How the hell do I deal with a dragon who likes to be in my personal space?"

"No, no, no. He's not a dragon. You'll see when we get there. You just have to show him who's boss." A toothy grin spread across Arius' face. "If nothing else is achieved, it should amuse me."

"Well, I'm glad I can offer you some entertainment," Sera grumbled.

He flickered a brief smile her way before turning solemn. "The thing is," Arius eyed her cautiously, seeming anxious about how she would react, "you need to work on controlling your talent, and we need to test it on someone other than myself." He paused and raised a claw to scratch behind his ear. "I figure that we can kill two birds with one stone. My friend can meet you and you can see if your powers work on him."

Worry sparked in her stomach, and the anxiety that she worked hard to keep trapped deep inside wormed its way up to grasp her by the throat. She placed a hand against the warm scales, drawing comfort, and centred herself.

"What if I can't control my power? What if he decides I'm a threat too? Your dragons didn't seem very happy about my abilities. What if I –"

"Hush." He snaked his head around and gently nudged her. "It will be okay. This is the best way to prepare ourselves for the arrival of the Council. My friend is going to love you, don't fret about him."

Ducking her head, she swallowed hard before admitting, "I'm scared."

"I will protect you," he murmured into her ear before suggesting, "Why don't you practise now?"

Sera nodded once, then relaxed into his side and let her head fall back. Her body rose each time he inhaled. Closing her eyes, she ran her thumb over the hilt of the knife at her hip, focusing on the feel of the staghorn handle, and allowed her mind to go blank. It was getting easier to transfer. She slipped into his thoughts, as easily as pushing past a curtain to see the view through a window.

I'm here.

That was quicker than last time. Well done!

Arius' delight in her improvement caused a bubble of happiness to bloom in her chest. She chastised herself for her desperate need to win his approval. She simply needed to learn how to control this strange power, gain the favour of the other dragons and return home. She didn't need his affection. She was frustrated that no matter how hard she tried to reject his friendship, his good opinion still held sway over her emotions.

Hopefully, it's enough control to appease your Council. Sera's thinly veiled jibe wasn't missed by Arius, whose thoughts turned melancholy.

Once again, I apologise for putting you in this position. But you have to understand, I have never experienced a power like yours, and I need to know that my trust in you is not foolish. The only way I can do that is to have others provide an unbiased and informed judgement on whether you could potentially harm dragonkind.

I keep telling you, I'm not out to hurt anyone. If she could roll her eyes at him, she would have.

Do you forget you are a Tracker? What if a dragon comes in between you and a mission objective one day? Are you telling me you wouldn't use this magic to stop the dragon?

I... I don't know. But I don't believe this is magic. No human I know can perform true magic. We use technology and science to make up for our lack of supernatural powers.

Arius snorted aloud. *Well, it's certainly not normal.*

Thanks for that. Nice to know we can agree on something.

Sera withdrew her consciousness from his mind abruptly. She felt a sense of loss when she cut her close contact with him, but pushed it aside. She didn't feel like being insulted. Especially by him.

"I'm sorry if I offen—" Arius opened his mouth as she stood up but she held up a finger to silence him.

"I'm going for a walk to practise on my own."

His tail nearly swept her feet out from under her as it brushed the boulder beneath them. "Don't go too far."

"Yeah, yeah, you can't afford to lose your precious prisoner, I get it."

The cheap shot made her feel better for a few seconds until she saw his face crumble at her words.

He quickly hid his face from her and murmured, "I merely meant to be careful of other predators. I'll stay out of your way. Please, call if you need me."

CHAPTER SIXTEEN

GUILT FOLLOWED HER AS she stalked away from Arius and into the bush. Each stride she took brushed ferns to the side, the dew that still clung to them from the previous night dripping onto her boots. She carefully picked her way over the tree roots that threatened to trip her. Arius' bulky form wouldn't be able to follow her through this tangle of forest without making a lot of noise. She marched away from the dragon, focussing on one step at a time as she tried to wrangle her anger into submission. While she walked, she absentmindedly rubbed the puckered pink skin on her arms that was the only reminder of her wounds from the night scamps. Ignoring the trills of bird song that filtered through the canopy, she pushed low branches away from her face and stepped into a clearing.

Eyeing off the small meadow warily, she skirted around the edge of it. She had no reason to suspect anything untoward, but her Tracker training was so ingrained that she had to do a quick scout before she could relax her guard. There was no sign of any tracks or strange smells. The birds were still singing, the sun was shining, and the soft grass invited her to sit and relax. She threw herself down and gazed into the endless sky. Unable to enjoy the tranquillity she frowned, berating herself for her spiteful comments. On the one hand, he had taken her against her will and called down a horde of dragons to decide whether she lived or died. On the other hand, he had helped her learn about her powers and had been exceedingly kind to her, for a dragon at least. As much as she didn't want to, she understood his point of view. If the tables were turned, she would be keeping him contained until she understood his potential threat towards her people too.

Sera sighed and rubbed at her eyes. *What am I supposed to do?*

Not be such a bitch about it would be a start.

Sera bolted upright, eyes wide. The voice was that of a stranger's, and not only that, was projected into her mind. This wasn't how her power worked, so she could only assume the person or mythic had their own abilities.

Who are you? Where are you?

All you have to do is close your eyes to see.

What in Ghaia's name does that mean?

If you're too stupid to figure that out I won't bother continuing this conversation. The foreign consciousness began to fade from her mind.

Wait!

Sera bit her lip and strained her eyes to see through the dense bush. There was nothing else for it, she'd have to chance it if she wanted to know who was speaking in her mind. Perhaps they could teach her more about her powers.

Going against all her instincts as a Tracker, she forced herself to relax. Placing her hand against Firinne, she quietened her thoughts. A bright spot flared in her mind's eye, a presence that she hadn't noticed when she entered the clearing.

Finally, said the stranger in her head. *Now, time for you to answer your own questions, who am I and where I am?*

How am I supposed to know that?

Seraphina, please prove to me that you're not as useless as the rest of your kind. Use your power. Feel my aura. See where I hide. Just try.

How do you know my name?

Tell me what I am, and I'll tell you how I know your name. Deal?

Fine.

Concentrating hard, Sera stroked Firinne again, running her fingertips along the patterns in the staghorn handle. Breathing deeply, she allowed her awareness to relax and stretch beyond her body. Her eyes were closed but she could still get a sense of her surroundings. Where she directed her thoughts, she noticed the same flares of light. They were various sizes, and she realised it was the life force of the creatures around her. The tiny pinpoints of brightness that climbed the trees were insects, the larger balls of light scurrying in the dirt were small rodents, and there, a few metres in from the clearing, but hiding up in the treetops, was that bright aura again. She directed her power, pushing her limits, and started to make sense of the shape.

Some sort of large cat? No, wait. You're a lynx!

Good... The voice purred in her head. *At least we now know that you're not totally useless. And I am where?*

You're up on a tree branch due south of where I am sitting.

Excellent. You show enough proficiency for me to trouble myself with your future. Stay where you are.

Sera sensed his feline form leap from the tree before she withdrew her mind back into herself. Shuddering on her hands and knees, she retched but had nothing in her stomach to bring up. Her body was shaking as if she'd just run a marathon. She managed to raise her head as the lynx appeared out of the shadows.

"I forgot to mention that side effect. Your mind is just like any other muscle; you need to train it. And at the beginning it will be hard work. With time and practise you will be able to push your thoughts further from you and See more. In the meantime, eat this." His black paw pushed a handful of purple berries towards her.

Where did he get them from? Frowning, she glanced at him, unsure whether to trust him enough to eat this strange fruit that he seemed to have pulled from thin air.

The lynx rolled his amber eyes skywards. "If I wanted you dead, I wouldn't waste my time poisoning you. I'd just rip your throat out. It doesn't really look like you're in a position to defend yourself." He drew his lips back to reveal his fangs in a feral smile.

"Touché," she managed to rasp out.

She hesitantly picked up a berry and sniffed it before placing it in her mouth. The burst of flavour coated her tongue, sweet and tart at the same time. She quickly wolfed down the rest of them when a rush of energy swept through her limbs. Pulling herself upright, she couldn't believe how much better she felt already.

"While you're discovering your magical abilities and limitations, I would recommend that you keep something sweet to eat nearby. In particular, these skyberries will aid in your recovery, but any fruit will suffice."

"Where do I find them?"

"They mainly grow in Sky Valley, but I wouldn't recommend visiting there unless you have a death wish. There are a few bushes scattered around here and there." He inclined his head back towards the waterfall.

"Thank you." Sera regarded him curiously, admiring his midnight fur that shone almost blue in the sun. Magical black flames flickered around his neck and along his spine. "Why are you helping me?"

"Tut, tut. I agreed to answer one question if you could find me, and it wasn't that one," the big cat reproached her. "Now, to the question of how I know your name. We've met before."

"We have? I feel like I would remember that."

He sat still, aside from twitching his tail and stared at her, his expression impassive.

"Hang on. You're not the lynx I saw a few weeks ago, are you? When I was out training?" she asked incredulously.

"Good to know you're not completely oblivious."

"I take it that's a 'yes' then?" She paused but when he didn't answer, continued, "That still doesn't answer the question of how you know my name."

"I entered your thoughts to confirm a suspicion I had."

"Well, that's rude."

"Says the girl who forced her way into a dragon's mind."

She glared at him. "How do you know about that? And what was the suspicion you wanted to check?"

"Tut, tut," he admonished once more. "I said I would answer one question. I've already said enough. One more piece of advice I will grant you. Trust only Arius. You will need his help to make it through the trials to come. You hold more power than you know."

"That's not cryptic at all," she said sarcastically.

"You're welcome." He smirked at her. Raising his gaze to the heavens, he sighed. "Fine. A non-cryptic instruction for you: it is imperative that you keep practising and gain full control of your magic."

A thrill raced up her spine at the word 'magic' but aloud she simply said, "Thank you for being specific." *Finally.*

I can hear your thoughts, silly girl.

She squeaked in shock. "Please show me how to use my... my magic."

Standing, the lynx stretched lazily. "Our powers differ in technique. Your best chance at success is to explore it further with your dragon. Oh, and one more thing. It's best if you keep the details of this conversation between us for now." He sauntered away from her with his flaming tail cocked at a jaunty angle before melting into the foliage.

"Wait! What do I do about the Council?"

She ran after him, but he had vanished. She paused under the canopy and scanned the ground in front of her for tracks. There was no sign the lynx had ever been there. She sent her awareness out and sensed the auras of small creatures nearby, but no flare of light revealed the mythic's location.

Confused, she returned to her position in the clearing and remained long after the lynx had left, pondering what he had shared with her.

Maybe I should run away. No doubt my life would be easier if I didn't have to deal with dragons and magic. I could hide in the forest. I'd survive. The feelings she tried to keep buried snaked their way out of their confines and whispered to her, *You don't really want to leave him. Your heart would shatter.*

She thrust the forbidden longing away. Doing her utmost to ignore her emotions, she contemplated her options. Intuition tugged at her thoughts, telling her that her power could make a positive change in the future of the human-mythic alliance. She felt the pressure of responsibility bubbling up inside her. The familiar feeling of anxiety wrapped its claws around her throat in a vice-like grip. Her breathing turned erratic and she rolled over onto her belly and screamed her frustration into the grass.

A sudden blast of wind above her head halted her panic attack and she threw herself out of the way, unsheathing her blade as she rolled to her feet. Bounding up into a fighting stance, she relaxed as quickly as she'd reacted when she saw it was Arius landing in the meadow.

Swinging his head in a wide arc, he demanded, "Have you been harmed? I heard you yell."

Shaking out her arms to ease the adrenaline coursing through her veins, she chuckled. "No, I'm fine. I was just having a mini-breakdown. I'm not hurt."

His growl echoed through the forest. "Don't scare me like that," he said as he shoved his face close to hers. His concern melted away her distress and she hugged him, her arms only reaching part of the way around his snout. Leaning her head against his warm scales, her fear of the future melted away.

He stiffened at the unexpected contact, before gruffly mumbling, "I am glad you are well." As she drew away, he sniffed curiously before wrinkling his nose in disgust. "You need another wash. You smell like cat."

CHAPTER SEVENTEEN

ALLEN AZURA WAS USUALLY a practical and mild-mannered man. Talented at blending into the environment, he excelled as a Tracker for the MRO. However, when he received the midnight call from Hazel all rationality fled. It didn't matter that Sera was a grown woman, and a gifted Tracker as well, she was still his little girl. And she was missing.

Panic gnawed at the edge of his thoughts, but years of practice allowed him to hold it at bay. So long as he had a plan, he would be able to control the dread that circled like a vulture. He'd spent the night making phone calls to arrange the search and then went for a walk to the stables to check in with Balthazar. The unicorn hadn't seen his daughter since their last training session and had immediately left to track her down. Allen was grateful for his assistance, pleased that Sera had such a strong bond with him. Leaving the stables just before first light, Allen strode into the foyer of the MRO, headed straight to the elevator and pressed the button for the top floor. The man he was going to see didn't go by a name, he was only known as the Director, and it was he who controlled the MRO with an iron fist. He had agreed to hold an emergency meeting for Allen at dawn.

After exiting the lift, he pressed his thumb to the touchscreen beside the door. His thumbprint was recognised by Frank, the AI that inhabited the building, and a disembodied voice announced his arrival to the Director. He fidgeted while waiting for the sliding doors to hiss open. He knew from experience that every moment counted when looking for a missing person, and all this waiting around was driving him crazy. All he wanted was to leave right now and seek out his daughter, but logically he knew he'd have a better chance of finding her with a systematic search by a team of qualified people.

Entering the sterile office, he wrinkled his nose at the scent of bleach. He'd heard rumours that the Director was obsessed with cleanliness and had his rooms deep cleaned daily. Casting a glance over the bare walls, he marched briskly to the glass desk that only had the man's desktop and mobile to clutter it.

"Tracker Allen," the man greeted him without turning away from the window that overlooked the empty training yard. A freshly pressed, dark grey suit covered an athletic body. His greying hair was shaved close to his head, affording him a military air. Keeping his hands clasped behind his back, he turned smartly to stare down Allen. The hard lines of the man's face were unreadable.

Ignoring the sharpness that stung his nose, Allen saluted. "Morning, Director, sir."

The broad-shouldered man nodded curtly. "So, you're here because your daughter is missing?"

"Yes, sir."

The Director opened his mouth to ask a question but paused when Frank's robotic voice came over the speaker. "Hunter Tyler to see you, sir."

"Admit him."

The doors hissed open and Sera's partnered Hunter entered.

He would never admit it out loud, but something about Tyler always irked Allen. The young man was a very capable Hunter by all accounts, and his family was well-known in the community. He couldn't put his finger on why, but he couldn't stand him. His feelings were validated when the Hunter swaggered in, seemingly oblivious to the tension in the room.

"Good morning, Director, Tracker Allen, sirs." He nodded respectfully to both men.

"Hunter Tyler," responded the Director. "Do you know why you're here?"

"Yes, sir. Tracker Allen called me last night."

"Good." He shifted his attention to Sera's father. "Please give us any information you have on her whereabouts."

"Sera was going on a camping trip for the weekend." Allen spoke like he was providing a report to his Hunter, reining his emotions in. "She goes hiking in the mountains by herself every couple of months. I think she mentioned something about hunting deer this trip to sell the skins to a shop. Again, nothing unusual for her. She spent much of her childhood in the wilds with me and, in my opinion, is an excellent Tracker. She's always very cautious and is never late back from her trips. This is abnormal behaviour for her. I contacted one of the guys from the IT department last night and he said he couldn't find the current location of her phone. The last place they could find its signal was four days ago, on her usual hiking trail in the Mandar Ranges. Something unusual must have happened." His voice broke and he struggled to check the tears that pricked at his eyes.

Tyler flashed a mocking glance in his direction before sobering his expression and addressing the Director. "In the year I've been working with Tracker Sera as my partner I have found this information to be correct, for the most part."

With a raised eyebrow, the Director queried, "For the most part?"

"I agree that she is an excellent Tracker, otherwise I wouldn't have chosen her as my partner. She's rarely late from gathering intel for my missions, and if she is, she always finds a way to communicate her updated plans to me. However, she has had incidents in the past where she's not been the most cautious. This may be one of those times."

Allen scowled at him while the Director brought her file up on his computer. "I see. I take it you're referencing the incident that resulted in her being suspended for a fortnight a few months ago?"

"Correct, sir."

"If we find her—" the Director corrected his sentence when he felt the Tracker's gaze burning into him. "Apologies. *When* we find her, she will be required to submit a full report of what happened in her absence. We may take disciplinary action if it is not in line with MRO's policies."

"Are you being serious?" His voice was incredulous. "My daughter may be fighting for her life right now, and all you're worried about is if she broke some rules while trying to survive."

"I understand your concern for your daughter's wellbeing," he growled, "but watch your tone with me, Tracker Allen, or you'll be facing suspension too." The Director turned to Tyler. "Your Tracker has been classed as missing for almost forty-eight hours now, so it's time to send out a search party. Most of our Hunter-Tracker partnerships are on other missions for the MRO, so we have limited manpower at this stage. I will grant you both permission to take a week's paid leave to look for her, along with your partnered Hunter, Allen. I hear you've already taken it upon yourself to send the unicorn Balthazar to search." A vein ticked in his temple. "I can't commit any further resources at this stage."

"So, that's it?" Allen demanded. "My girl is missing and all you can spare is three people and a unicorn?"

"It's not the first time this has happened, and it won't be the last. I'm sure she'll turn up. They usually do. I refuse to make an exception to our standard procedure this early in the investigation. I will review the situation in forty-eight hours and assign further assistance if necessary."

A phone rang. The Director stilled and his face tightened. Reaching into his vest pocket, he pulled out a second mobile and pressed it to his ear.

"Yes, sir? You've heard about it already? Tracker Seraphina Azura... I see... Right away, sir."

Perplexed, Allen shot a glance at Tyler who looked just as puzzled as he was.

Carefully placing the phone back in his inner pocket, the Director stared coldly at him. "It's your lucky day, Tracker Allen. We will be adding another team of eight to the search party, and in a few days, one of the helicopters will be made available to seek your daughter. The President has taken a special interest in the case."

CHAPTER EIGHTEEN

ANOTHER NIGHT PASSED FOLLOWING the same pattern of eating simple food and talking to Arius. They spoke for hours about everything and nothing. She explained how her father had raised her and about her close bond with Balthazar. She described her friend and flatmate Hazel and their home on the twenty-eighth floor in the Mandar City Apartments. As the sun rose to welcome a new morning, Sera lay on her bed of furs and reflected on the past six days. The feelings of confusion reigned supreme when she thought of the dragon that had initially abducted and terrified her. Everything had changed now. They shared a quiet breakfast of bird eggs and pork from a boar he had killed, before taking to the skies once again. Despite his reassurances, a tingle of nervousness wound up her spine as she prepared to meet his mysterious friend.

After a brief scout of the area, they landed on the plateau. It was only a short flight from his home to the flat ground that cut into the mountainside above the cave. From out of the trees that lined the open space a strange creature appeared. Shielding her eyes from the sun, Sera watched as he cantered toward them. He had the body of a horse and the wings and head of an eagle. A hippogryph. She exhaled in relief. She had enjoyed the friendship of the hippogryph who had taught her at MINATH. She walked toward the striking mythic as he trotted closer, and when his attention was on her, she dropped her eyes to the ground and slowly stepped back, inviting him into her space. Black hooves appeared at the top of her vision and a dappled grey shoulder barged into hers.

"Ooompf!" she exclaimed as she found herself on the ground. Yellow eyes that danced with merriment gazed into hers before the hippogryph lowered his head and nudged her with his beak.

"Not the first time a woman has been swept off her feet by my animal magnitude." The hippogryph wiggled his feathery eyebrows at her, full of cheek.

A low rumbling chuckle from behind Sera answered his unorthodox introduction. "Seraphina, this is my friend, Torvold," Arius announced. "Torvold, Seraphina."

Torvold's head swivelled quickly to scrutinise Arius. "Seraphina, eh? That's an interesting name."

"You can call me Sera," she said as she stood up and dusted off her pants.

Turning back towards her, he winked and said, "And you, my sweet, can call me Tor."

"Well, I'd say it's nice to meet you Tor, but most gentlemen I know don't knock ladies to the ground." She raised an eyebrow back at him.

"Oh, she gives the sass back! Good girl!" He swished his tail happily and fluffed his feathers. "You need some practice in the noble art of wordplay, but you'll get there, my sweet. Many friends of mine are just so dull and don't know how to spar with words and it's one of my favourite pastimes. Aside from wooing you, of course." He sidled closer.

Sera's mouth dropped open at his brazen behaviour and she glanced back at Arius in bewilderment. She returned her eyes to Torvold and searched his face to figure out whether he was joking, unsure whether to laugh or smack him. She decided on the latter. In a quick movement, she spun past his shoulder, along his side and landed a sharp slap on his rump.

"Don't be rude," she admonished him with a grin.

"I deserved that." He opened his beak in an approximation of a smile before turning to Arius. "I like her."

Another chuckle came from Arius as he rolled his eyes at his friend. "I am glad she has your approval. But before you get ahead of yourself, I need your help."

Tor dropped his knees into the dirt and lowered his feathered head into a bow. "I am your humble servant, as always, dear friend."

"Stop showing off and stand up," Arius huffed. "This is a serious matter. We don't have time for your theatrics."

"My apologies. How can I be of assistance?" Tor cocked his head, his movements quick as he stood once more.

"It appears that Seraphina has the ability to enter my mind at will. I called a Dragon Council to ascertain if she is a threat to our way of life." He bowed his head and shifted his weight anxiously. "However, I feel I may have been too hasty in doing so. I fear that they will not listen to reason and will demand her execution." He ignored Sera's intake of breath and continued, "I need us to go into the meeting with as much information as possible, and for Seraphina to learn as much as she can about her powers in the short amount of time we have before the dragons arrive."

Tor's eyes narrowed. "How long do you have?"

"Two more days."

He clicked his beak open and shut a few times in apparent distress. "You weren't joking when you said we didn't have time for my theatrics. All right, how can I help Sera?"

"We need to know if her power extends to other mythics, or if she can only enter the minds of dragons."

Sera placed a gentle hand on Tor's wither, just in front of his wings. "I'm asking permission to attempt to enter your mind, Tor. I understand if you would rather keep your thoughts from me, and I won't be upset if you choose not to open your mind to me."

"You didn't ask my permission," Arius grumbled quietly in the background.

Tor turned his head so one eye was level with hers and brushed her shoulders with his feathery wingtips. "The way I see it, it's a case of life and death, my sweet. I am willing to assist you in this matter. I'm ready when you are."

Sera found a comfortable spot on the ground and settled in before closing her eyes and concentrated on steadying her breathing. She was finding it easier to slip into the meditative state needed to access her power. Casting out with her consciousness, she felt Arius behind her. Ignoring him, she extended a tendril of thought towards the strange mind in front of her.

Hello, Tor? Can you hear me?

There was no response. She sensed Tor's warm aura in front of her, but it was so foreign that she couldn't gain entry to his thoughts. Frowning in concentration, she widened her focus. She quickly realised there were tiny pinpricks of consciousness at her feet and recognised it was a line of ants. Pushing further out, past Arius, she could feel the hawks that rose on the columns of air blowing off the mountain's ridges. Her mind followed the trail of small lights that surrounded her and found the mice that burrowed in their tunnels, the beetles that climbed the trees and, very faintly, the remains of the colony of night scamps that hid in the heart of the mountain. The points of golden light lit up her mind, each representing a life, and created a rich tapestry that blanketed the world she thought she knew and left her gasping in awe. Unexpectedly, her mind recoiled like the twang of a bowstring and she snapped back into herself. She tried to open her eyes but her body wouldn't obey. She felt herself falling, as if from a great height, until the black abyss swallowed her up.

It seemed like an age had passed before Sera managed to open her eyes briefly. The concerned faces of Arius and Tor peered down at her, then a wave of dizziness forced her to squeeze them shut again. The solid earth against her back felt like the only thing that was stopping her from slipping back into the void. Dimly, she heard her name being shouted from far away. It echoed through her brain, seeming to bounce around like it was the only word that existed. Shuddering, she opened her eyes, pulled herself onto her elbow and retched. Bile coated her tongue and made her gag. A talon gently cradled her body and the comforting pressure grounded her, stopping the world from spinning.

"Seraphina! Can you hear me?" Arius' worried voice finally broke through the fog.

"Yes," she croaked out.

"Here, eat this." He pushed a pile of berries towards her.

She started to eat, the sweet juices running down her chin, and the same rush of energy pulsed through her. "Where did you find skyberries?" she asked.

Before Arius could answer, Tor was in her face, waggling his eyebrows as he said, "That's for him to know, and you to find out!"

Arius used his snout to nudge Tor out of his way, his head the size of the hippogryph's entire body. "Sera, are you all right? What happened?"

"I'm not exactly sure..." She frowned, gazing out over the cliff, noting the hawks that hovered there. "I think I exhausted myself by pushing too far away from my body."

"You connected with Tor?" Arius exclaimed.

"No," she began, and Tor shook his feathered head, "I couldn't enter his mind. But I could sense his aura. Along with the ants, the hawks, the mice..." She stared around the plateau as she struggled to gather her wits. "I could feel the presence of all the life around me. But you were the only one whose mind I could have connected with. It seems I can only communicate with you... or dragons, I guess. But I can detect the presence of other lifeforms near me."

"That is curious. At least we know now. Thank you for agreeing to assist us, Torvold." Arius nodded in gratitude to the hippogryph.

"It was my pleasure." Tor returned the bow before sweeping a wing around the now upright Sera. "You take care of this girl, Arius. I have a feeling she is going to be the catalyst of great change in our world. I must return to my flock now, Sera. Fly well, my sweet!"

Tor winked at her, nudged her cheek with his beak, and then cantered towards the edge of the cliff and leapt, flinging himself into the air. His huge wingspan caught an updraft and he soared into the clouds, disappearing quickly from sight.

Arius turned his great head to Sera. "I do have to ask, how do you know about skyberries?"

Dropping her eyes, Sera hesitated. The lynx hadn't wanted her to tell Arius about their meeting. Peeking up at the great scaled head that hovered over her, she gave him a mischievous smile and used Tor's words. "That's for me to know, and you to find out."

CHAPTER NINETEEN

UPON RETURNING TO THE cave, Arius gave her a strange look.

She squirmed, uncomfortable under his intense scrutiny. "What's the matter?"

"Do you trust me, Seraphina?"

It was a loaded question, but she answered without hesitation. "I do. I know I probably shouldn't, but I can't help it. All of my Tracking training is shouting for me to escape, race back to the MRO and report you, but sometimes... sometimes it's more important to follow your heart than your head."

"I know precisely what you mean." He murmured the words so softly she wasn't sure she was supposed to hear. "Wait here, I have something to show you." He marched to the back of the cave with his wings folded tensely against his back and disappeared behind the boulder.

Half an hour passed and Sera waited at the edge of the cave, enjoying the changing colours of the sky. The sun was heading westward and was hidden behind the mountain, casting long shadows on the countryside before her. Alarm slammed into her chest when she heard the echo of footsteps on the rocky floor behind her. A man was walking through the cave.

A man! She slipped quietly behind the closest stalagmite and examined him as he stopped beside the fire pit in the centre of the cavern. *What in Ghaia's name is happening?*

Only a few days ago, she would have been screaming for him to help her escape this place but now she didn't know what she wanted after all that Arius had done for her. He'd protected her, cared for her, and had become a true friend. Her feelings for him went against everything she'd ever been taught. By MINATH, by the MRO, and even by her father. She trusted Arius, and she was certain he had begun to trust her. Her feelings were a jumble, but she knew her mind enough to know she wasn't ready to leave him yet. Hopefully, this stranger hadn't noticed her.

How did he get in here? And where is Arius?

She studied him from the shadows, noticing the smooth tan skin that covered a muscular body. His wild, coffee-coloured hair flowed past his broad shoulders and a short beard covered his face. Soft moss-green trousers covered his long legs but otherwise, he was bare-chested and barefoot. He raised his eyes and stared directly at her. She froze, pinned to the spot as time stood still. She knew those emerald eyes. She had been staring into them for the past week. This wasn't possible. The man smiled at her and approached cautiously, with his hands held wide, palm up to show he was unarmed.

Stopping a few metres from her, he greeted her in a familiar voice. "Hello, Seraphina."

Her jaw dropped. *It can't be.* The deep honeyed tones stirred her heart into hyper-drive. Her eyes darted to his bare chest and she saw a scar across the collarbone. The same place it was on Arius.

"Who... How are you..." she stammered, her voice trailing off in confusion.

The familiar eyes and the same warm voice enveloped her. "It's all right," he whispered gently, stretching a hand toward her, treating her like a frightened animal.

How is Arius in human form?

None of the history books she'd read had mentioned that dragons could shift into human form. Her knees trembled, the shock causing her legs to buckle. He was beside her in a flash, supporting her weight as she sank against the wall.

"It's all right," he repeated, brushing her hair back from her temple as he settled on the ground beside her. That one simple touch triggered an electric hum through her body.

"I don't understand," Sera managed to choke out.

"Dragons are all born with a special talent. A form of magical ability specific to that dragon. Some can control the weather, some can shape the earth, and others, such as myself, have the ability to shift forms. My talent is that I can transform into a human. I don't particularly enjoy it as I much prefer my natural state; however, it has proven useful in the past." His arm was around her shoulders, his body unnaturally warm, but the shivers coming from her were no longer from the shock of seeing him in human form.

"That's... unbelievable." She shook her head in amazement.

"I realise it's a lot to take in. Allow me to prove it to you. Why don't you enter my mind?"

"Will I still be able to? Considering you're a human?"

The man – Arius – frowned. "Good point. I hadn't thought of that. Give it a try anyway. It will be a good test, regardless. And if it doesn't work, I will just shift back into my true form and you can see for yourself."

Sera tried to relax and ignore the prickles of heat running along her shoulders where his arm rested against her. Slipping into her now-familiar meditative state, she let her mind expand. Almost immediately, she snapped into Arius' consciousness.

Hello, Arius? Is that truly you?

Yes. Amusement coloured his thoughts. *I am in my human form. I wanted to show you... for you to know me... all of me. I wanted to offer you my trust.*

Thank you, she whispered as she withdrew from his mind.

He smiled gently at her, his eyes crinkling. It was hard to guess his age; his body was in its prime, and his face looked to be that of a thirty-year-old. His eyes though... she could lose herself in their ancient depths.

"I don't quite know what to say," she stammered.

"It's okay," he murmured, rubbing calloused fingers over her shoulders. "I know it's a surprise. I am sorry I didn't reveal myself to you sooner. I did not trust you. I see now that I should have. Please accept my sincerest apologies." His words were genuine and heartfelt.

Sera blushed at the intensity of his gaze. She peeked up under her lashes at his face. A small smile bared his perfectly normal human-shaped teeth. He caught the direction of her stare and ran his tongue along his flat teeth.

"I will admit, aside from the lack of wings, this is one of the most uncomfortable aspects of being in human form. I miss my fangs."

She stared at him for a moment, unsure how to react, before a bubble of laughter burst out. The incredible creature that was Arius boggled her mind, but the mirth put a stop to the hysteria that threatened to overwhelm her.

He's still my dragon, just in a different skin.

She turned her body toward him and reached forward hesitantly, her hand hovering just above the skin of his chest. His hand enveloped hers and pulled it towards him. She bit back a yelp as her hand connected with his body and a vibration thrummed through her veins. She felt his heart beating, far slower than was normal for a human. Her eyes lingered on his lips, wondering what it would be like to kiss them. His right hand cupped her jaw and his thumb grazed her cheek. The spark in her blood electrified into something far more intense as his eyes raked over her body hungrily. Fear clouded her mind. Not fear of what he would do to her, nor was it fear of what people would think. It was a fear that he would take her and find her lacking. Her heart wouldn't survive the rejection if he decided she wasn't enough for him. Admitting that to herself made her feel as if she had betrayed everyone who had ever put their trust in her as a Tracker. She wasn't supposed to feel this way about a mythic. Especially one that had abducted her. Her tangled thoughts made her head spin, even as her body was drawn to him.

Sera swiftly extricated herself from his hold and stood, dusting her pants off. Bewilderment briefly flickered over Arius' face, but he rearranged his features quickly into an easy smile.

"I can appreciate the strangeness of the situation for you. Please, if you have any questions, I would be happy to answer them."

Still flustered from his closeness, Sera said the first thing that popped into her head, "Can you still breathe fire in this form?"

Arius chuckled. "Sadly, no. Although that would be something, eh?" He winked at her, a lock of his brown hair falling over his forehead and accentuating his roguish appearance.

He's not making this easy. Gods, he is attractive.

She rubbed her hands over her face as she paced away from him. With a bit of luck, if she avoided looking him in the eye, she could wrestle her wayward thoughts into submission. Concentrating on the uneven rock at her feet, she thought about her next, hopefully less asinine, question.

"How does a dragon's talent form? As in, is it a genetic thing? Oh Gods, please tell me your father can't change into a human?" She blanched at that, panicking about the havoc Talegar could wreak in Mandar City as a man.

"No, no, it's nothing like that." Arius' soothing voice was closer than she expected and she flinched. "His talent is vastly different from mine. To my knowledge, I am the only dragon currently alive who has this particular ability."

His hand grasped her shoulder firmly and turned her to face him. Sera had planned to keep her eyes trained forward and ignore his beguiling face but now she was forced to examine his broad chest. The muscles rippled and flexed as if aching to be freed of the constraints of the delicate skin and to burst forth into scaled armour.

"How did you get that scar?" she asked as she traced her finger along the old wound.

He shuddered at her caress. "I fought another dragon. We rarely fight amongst ourselves, but when we do, it is a terrible thing to behold. I was blessed to not have been injured more severely."

"What were you fighting about?"

He paused for so long she didn't think he was going to answer. When he did it was a whisper. "About the death of my mother."

"Oh! I'm so sorry. I shouldn't have asked." Sera cast her eyes down.

He held her jaw and tilted her chin gently up, forcing her to look at him. "Don't be sorry."

His gaze hovered on her lips before rising to meet her sapphire eyes. She could see a question in the swirling emerald irises, but she couldn't bring herself to voice her answer. She trembled as he leant forward. He rested his forehead against hers and closed his eyes, peace travelling across the planes of his face. Their breath mingled together as they stood together in silence, taking comfort in each other's presence.

Too soon, Arius drew himself away with a reluctant smile. "I have to change back. I use up a lot of energy if I stay human for too long. Please excuse me." He bowed low.

Sera giggled at the medieval gesture but delighted in it anyway.

Stepping away from her, his eyes glinting with mischief, he flashed a grin. "Are you ready for this?"

"Ready for wh-" She broke off with a shriek as he sprinted towards the cave's mouth.

Leaping into the abyss, his human form exploded as massive wings unfurled from his shoulders and scales and spines erupted from his skin. His face elongated, talons bloomed from his fingers and a tail sprouted from his body. Thundering a challenge to the heavens, the copper dragon turned his massive head towards Sera as he hovered in front of her. Her mouth hung open, awestruck, as she took it all in.

"That. Was. Epic!"

CHAPTER TWENTY

STANDING AT THE CAVE'S entrance, Sera stared into the gloomy night sky. It had been a whole day since he had revealed his human form to her. They had spent the past twenty-four hours roaming the mountain, Arius alternating between human and dragon form. Together, they had explored her abilities, and she was feeling slightly more prepared for the impending interrogation. Every moment spent with him cemented her feelings for him further.

Squalls of rain drove sheets of water into the cave's entrance, coating everything in inescapable dampness. She stood still, just out of range, watching the rivulets of water gathering on the ground. The weather suited her mood. The fear of tomorrow's meeting tore at her heart, threatening to overpower her resolve.

"It's a full moon tonight," she announced quietly.

"I know." Arius' voice was heavy. "The Council will meet us on the plateau tomorrow at first light. I will fly you up there. Do not fear, I will support you. You have learned to control your talent quickly; it's quite remarkable. They cannot fault your desire to master your power. We will find a way to make them understand that you are not a threat. Come, Seraphina. Let us share one night of peace without worrying about what tomorrow will bring."

He knelt and boosted her onto his back with his fore-leg. They dove into the storm clouds that shrouded the mountain, each stroke of his copper wings pushing the dreary night away. She shook the front of her jacket to try to disperse the water droplets that slid down the leather. She inhaled the fresh scent of the storm, the sharpness filling her lungs. She couldn't see a thing through the fog but the crisp air invigorated her body, making her blood hum.

Arius adjusted his flight and rose higher, bursting through the ceiling of the cloud cover and into the clear sky. Sera gasped as the misty world fell away. The full moon's soft glow illuminated the tops of the clouds, painting them in shades of silver. The colour leeched from their bodies, creating a black and white scene as they sailed through the moonlit sky. In the distance, flashes of lightning lit up the sky. She leant over the dragon's neck to look at the sea of clouds, longing to stretch a hand down and run her fingers through them.

He continued to rise into the heavens, soaring towards the glowing orb. The bitter wind chilled her, raising pebbles along her arms, even through her clothing. The heat that always burned within Arius soaked into her, warming her freezing body as she rested her head against his scales. Turning her face, she pressed her lips to his skin, thawing the ice crystals that coated them. A contented rumble resonated from deep within him. Blinking the frost from her eyelashes, she frowned as she concentrated on a faint melody.

She projected her thoughts into Arius' mind. What is that? It sounds like... like a song. But like no song I've ever heard.

That's Illundar. Or starsong in your tongue.

Starsong? I've never heard of it!

That's because humans don't normally fly this high without the assistance of noisy machines. If your kind listened more, they would discover all manner of secrets.

So what exactly is Illi... starsong?

Exactly what it's called. The song of the stars.

Stars sing?

He chuckled softly. *Yes. I forget that, while we may share the same world, you know so little of what exists outside your city.*

Teach me?

It would take centuries to tell you everything. But I will try.

She had always assumed that science and technology had overtaken the magic of the mythics. She'd thought that any mystery remaining had faded from the world along with the dragons. A sense of wonder glowed in her soul every time Arius taught her about the magic that still inhabited the earth. They glided through the air on noiseless wings in companionable silence, both lost in their respective thoughts. She could easily forget about her old world, cocooned in this bubble of magic. Time spun out between them like a spool of thread, tenuous and fragile. She wished she could stay in this moment with him forever.

Arius?

Yes, Seraphina?

I... I just wanted to say... I'm glad.

Glad? For what?

That you took me. That you helped me. That you... befriended me.

Oh, Seraphina. His tone was wretched. *I feel such remorse for taking you away from your life. If I could go back... I would change everything. Though I will admit that I am selfish enough to be glad of your friendship too. I feel guilty for enjoying your company too much. I'm terrified of losing you. And of the fact that it's inevitable. No matter what the Council decides tomorrow, I will lose you. Either back to your old life. Or by...*

He let the sentence hang between them, not wanting to say the word, 'execution.' She forced the dread away that tried to take control of her thoughts.

There's always more than two options.

What do you mean?

That's something my dad always said... whenever you think you're backed against the wall, there's always another way.

Your father sounds like a wise man.

He is. I miss him.

I will do everything in my power to ensure that you are returned to him safely.

Can you do me a favour, Arius?

Anything.

If... If I do die... please make sure my body is returned to him. He'll spend his whole life searching for me if I never come home, and I don't want him to end up in danger on my account.

His wingbeats grew heavy with melancholy but he nodded. *I will. I swear it.*

CHAPTER TWENTY-ONE

THE STARS BEGAN TO wink out of existence as night gradually gave way to the dawn. The full moon had disappeared behind the mountain and the sun threatened to burst over the eastern horizon at any moment. Arius snorted softly to rouse Sera, but she was already awake. Her eyes felt like sandpaper every time she blinked.

After they returned from their flight, sleep had eluded her for most of the night as she played out potential scenarios. *I have to make them see I have control. I'm not a threat to them.* She moved to his side and stared out over the vista, laying her hand against his scaled cheek. He hummed deep in his throat in an attempt to soothe her and leaned into the contact. The now-familiar tug low in her abdomen returned, and she gave up trying to fight it. Turning towards him, she buried her face against his and sobbed. Releasing the silent heaves seemed to offer a type of healing in itself. Arius rested the end of his tail on her shoulders and pressed her to his cheek.

"It will be all right," he rumbled. "I won't let them hurt you." A tremor ran through his body as he murmured, "I'm sorry. I shouldn't ha—" his voice broke, "I should never have called the Council. If I had known..." He trailed off and pulled himself away from her, a grim set to his mouth. "Come. We must go now."

Arius flew them to the plateau as the sky lightened above them. His talons dug into the dirt, softening the impact of his landing. Sera leapt from his back and swept the area, looking for any potential escape routes or makeshift weapons, should it come to that.

A cliff face, a heap of rocks, a few trees and a few thousand-foot drop on the other side. Great.

She peered upwards, desperately trying to locate the dragons coming to decide her fate and felt the pressure in her ears before she saw them. Three great dark shapes materialised from the shadows of the land below them. Their wings beat in unison and an almost unbearable thumping in her head drove her to her knees. Even through the pain in her eardrums she could admire their majesty. Dragons of the sun, the moon and the night. They were even more impressive in the flesh. Arius quickly wrapped a wing around her to protect her from the miniature whirlwind that sprung into being as the dragons alighted in front of them.

Thank you, she whispered into his mind and pressed a hand against his warm body before straightening up and stepping forward to greet them.

Sera couldn't control the shiver that ran through her body at the proximity of the enormous mythics. Arius was at her back, the golden dragon faced her and the other two sat on either side of her, closing off any hope of escape.

Bowing low, she kept her eyes fixed on the ground as she said, "Greetings. I am Seraphina Azura of Mandar

City, friend to Arius, and I stand before you, offering my respect, and I trust that you will offer me the same."

A low growl came from the dragon to her left, the black, as his tail thrashed aggressively. Ignoring her fear, Sera kept her eyes trained on the ground until a talon appeared in front of her. The white dragon on her right gently pressed the flat of her claw under Sera's chin and lifted her face. They gazed at each other, and Sera marvelled at her beauty. Arius' sister shared his emerald eyes and the same kind expression. Her neck was slender, her face elegant. She wasn't truly white; every scale appeared to have been carved from opals and rainbows danced over her body when the light caught her movement.

"Well met, Seraphina. I am Aliah of Sky Valley and I greet you with an open heart." Her voice was soft and musical, and Sera took an immediate liking to her.

Aliah stepped back in deference to the golden dragon as his piercing stare pinned Sera in place. He was the largest of the four with scales that shone like the sun itself. It almost hurt to look at him.

His booming voice filled the air. "Well met, indeed. I am Talegar of Sky Valley, and I come to hear your plea and vow to pass fair judgement."

A feral growl ripped from the throat of Arius' brother and his obsidian wings snapped open, making him appear even larger. He snarled at his father, "Fair judgement? Let us kill her now and be done with this charade. She is a human, and with the MRO at that. She doesn't deserve a trial. Our mother didn't get one before being murdered by this human's brethren."

Sera felt rather than saw a tremor run through Arius, while Aliah flinched as if she'd been struck.

Talegar kept his golden orbs trained on Sera while he spoke to his son. "Desamor, if you cannot remain impartial before we hear the evidence, you will be removed from this Council."

The hiss that came from Desamor's mouth chilled Sera to her very core. She projected her thoughts into Arius. *He holds so much hate for me already. Why? And what happened to your mother?*

I will explain later. Arius glared at his brother, wrinkling back his lips to bare his fangs.

"The same goes to you, Arius," his father reminded him. "You must not be swayed by any regard you feel towards your... pet."

He paused a moment as if waiting for one of his sons to interject. Aside from a twitch from Arius when his father called her his pet, he remained silent. Both dragons bowed their heads in submission.

"Let us begin.

"Arius has told us how he found you, and that you invaded his mind in your sleep without his permission. The last we heard, you had no control over this ability, and Arius couldn't forcibly remove you from his consciousness. Has this information changed?"

Arius stepped forward, using his foreleg to shield Sera, as he answered, "Seraphina and I have been exploring her boundaries and her control has exceeded expectations. She has the abili—"

"ARIUS!" Talegar interrupted with a bellow. "Seraphina has a tongue. She can answer for herself. She is the one on trial here, not you."

Sera discerned magic lacing his words, but the energy wasn't directed at her. The power that fell from his tongue crashed into Arius and forced him to his knees. Sera screamed and ran to his head, running her hands desperately along his snout.

"What have you done to him?" she yelled at Talegar. "Stop it!" She stepped in front of his nose and, threading all of her energy into her words, shouted, "I SAID STOP!"

The magic cut off. Arius grunted, and scrambled back onto his feet, eyes wide as he stared at Sera.

"Well. That is interesting." Talegar cocked his head, scrutinising her. "Very interesting. The floor is yours, Seraphina. Please, share with us the new evidence pertaining to your strange abilities."

The way he spoke made her shudder, his voice dripping like poisoned honey. The words were said kindly but there was a subtle undercurrent of violence. This was not a dragon to be trifled with.

She glanced back at Arius to check that he had recovered, before turning to answer his father. "As Arius began to tell you, we have been practising over the past week. Before meeting him I didn't know I had any special ability. I can now control when I enter his mind and can regulate the level of control I have within. I can get a sense of his aura now without actually entering his mind, and I can project my thoughts into his to communicate and hear his response. I stay connected to my own body during these exchanges and can still move and speak as normal. I can also go a level deeper and share his senses, in that I can see, hear, feel, smell and taste all that he experiences, however, I lose control of my own body. Distance doesn't seem to be an issue although it is easier to make the transfer if I'm touching him."

"Have you ever gone a level deeper?" The gaze of Arius' father was so intense she thought she would burst into flame at any moment.

Puzzled, she asked, "A level deeper? What do you mean?"

Talegar's face was so close all she would have to do was lean forward and she would touch him. "Have you ever taken over control of his body?"

A sick feeling settled in her stomach at his words and bile rose in her throat. She managed to spit out the words. "I would never... I could never do that. That would be... wrong. So wrong." She shook her head vehemently.

Talegar sighed and leaned back. The release of tension that came with him leaving her personal space made her knees weak. "That is comforting to hear," he said, but the way he said it suggested he felt otherwise.

She could see the calculating look and sense the way his mind worked. She didn't trust him.

"But it is one thing to claim you can do something and quite another to actually do it. If you will, please perform a demonstration for us?"

"What... what do you mean?"

"Try to enter my mind. Hear my thoughts, if you can."

She looked to Arius for support. He nudged her gently and whispered, "Do as he says."

"If you insist." She closed her eyes and breathed.

CHAPTER TWENTY-TWO

SHE SENSED THE INTIMIDATING presence of the four dragons surrounding her; she got the impression of Desamor's aura being as dark as Aliah's was light, but she ignored them for the time being. The familiarity of Arius' thoughts pulled her towards him but she ripped herself away and turned her attention to the beast in front of her. His aura was grey, with dark ribbons ripping parts of the light into shreds. Breathing evenly, she eased herself into his thoughts and felt him throw a thick stone wall up to shield his mind. But she was like the wind, and finding the cracks in the stone, slipped through easily. She discerned his surprise at her ability to break through his mental defences so quickly.

He was centuries old with a mind so vast she thought she might get lost in its depths. He was a master strategist with many schemes that would alter depending on the outcomes of others. His plans looked like spools of thread that ran through his mind, crisscrossing through each other, joining together in some places and splitting off in others.

She already felt sick about being inside his consciousness, so she chose not to study the threads, instead whispering, *Talegar, I am here, as requested. Can you hear me?*

A low growl echoed around her, reverberating from the far reaches of his mind. *Yes. I did not expect you to succeed. But since you are here, and seeing as you are on trial, I need to understand the depth of your power. I need you to go a level deeper.*

I don't want to do that.

Do as I command, or I will not hesitate to order your execution.

She gulped in fear and did as he bid.

Talegar's ancient mind was so complex that it quickly became clear it was not as simple to delve into the next layer as it was with Arius. Sera examined her surroundings more closely. She drifted along on the currents of his mind, like a leaf on a river, making her way towards a bright light in the centre of his consciousness. Images floated to the surface of his thoughts, flowing past too quickly for her to fully grasp their meaning. There was a baby dragon, copper in colour, snuggled up beside Talegar. A battlefield covered in pools of blood of humans and mythics alike. A stunning warrior dragon, whose scales sparkled like diamonds, fell from the air, a bloody hole in her chest. Other moments flashed past, too fast to make any sense. One last image sprung forth of a beautiful sapphire dragon diving into a perfectly round lake before Sera fell into the next level of the dragon's mind.

Breathing quickly, she peered around her. Sera could see her unconscious form on the ground in front of the dragons, with Arius standing over her body defensively. She could feel the wind murmur over Talegar's spines and the sun at their back beginning to warm his golden scales. She sensed his magic stirring within him in response to her presence, but he held it at bay. Aliah inspected her father closely and gasped.

"Father, your eyes have changed colour. They're almost blue." Aliah's voice was alive with curiosity, but Desamor began pacing uneasily at the revelation.

"She has joined minds with me." Talegar pushed out the words and shuddered, the foreign feeling of her presence distressing him.

"Is she attacking you?" demanded Desamor. "I knew we couldn't trust her!"

"No. Her presence in my mind... it makes me ill at ease. But she is not attacking me."

"How do we know that it is you speaking to us? Could she not have overtaken your mind?" raged the black dragon.

"That's enough, Desamor. You will be quiet."

This time the compulsion was aimed at his middle child. Sera felt the familiar way Talegar pulled his magic from the well within him but she couldn't access the ethereal wisps of power. The black dragon's head dropped to the ground in submission.

I can't affect your speech, Talegar. Or touch your magic. I can only absorb the senses you experience from the outside world. I can see this scene in front of us, hear what they are saying, feel the warmth of the sun on our scales, smell the fresh dirt under our talons, taste the fear from Desamor. I swear to you, I am not a threat.

You intrigue me, human.

It's Seraphina.

Talegar snarled, *I am your superior and hold your future in my talons. I will call you what I wish.*

Sera shivered as her fear of Talegar mingled with his hatred towards her, their emotions blending with the barriers lowered between their minds.

I need to know if you can control a dragon's mind.

I told you, I can't do that.

Can't or won't? he growled. *I command you to attempt to go a level deeper into my subconscious. Try to control me.*

No.

He snarled at her defiance and, leaping forward, smashed his son out of the way and grabbed her limp body. He called on his talent, using it to freeze Arius in place. The aggression rolling off his intellect directed towards her was powerful. Sera felt the spark of his magic entwining with his animosity.

You will do as I say. Or I will end your life with one slice.

Through his eyes, she watched as he raised a claw to threaten her exposed neck. Her consciousness began quivering uncontrollably.

What are you doing? he demanded.

It seems Arius' theory was right. If my physical body feels threatened, I can't maintain the connection.

With that, she was catapulted violently from his thoughts, threads of lights and images darting past her in a blur. She had a moment of peace as she realised she had made it safely back to her body, but before she could open her eyes, a shadowy curtain overtook her thoughts and she passed out.

CHAPTER TWENTY-THREE

SHE WAS CONSCIOUS. SHE knew that much. But she couldn't muster the will to open her eyes. She held onto the comforting warmth that surrounded her body, desperately trying to find her way back to gain control of her senses. A fiery line of heat traced along her jaw.

Arius...

She struggled violently against the darkness still claiming her body. Taking in a rattling breath, her eyes flew open to find anxious whirlpools of green in a human face. Arius met her gaze and cried out in relief.

Pressing his face into her shoulder he murmured, "Thank the Gods. I was afraid I had lost you." He kept his head buried in her neck, lips brushing her skin.

At that point, Sera became aware that she was lying in his lap and his arms encircled her body. Heat radiated off his body in pulses. She blushed as her body automatically reacted to his closeness and the touch of his skin against hers.

Arius continued, oblivious to her reaction, "I thought... I thought that you had been overpowered by my father's compulsion and would never regain your senses. You've been unconscious for an entire day. I would never forgive myself if he had taken your spirit away when it was I who called him here."

Grief tore at his features. A part of her heart broke at his anguish and she hesitantly reached her hand up to smooth the furrows in his brow.

"Hush. It's okay. I'm fine. Just hungry." She chuckled weakly.

"Here. Eat these." He shoved some skyberries at her.

She chewed quickly, the energy returning to her limbs.

He turned his cheek and pressed his face into her palm. He kissed each finger delicately before wrapping her arm around his neck and picking her up.

"I have to show you something." Each step rubbed his arms against her, leaving a part of her wishing the thin layer of clothing that separated them didn't exist. He walked to the back of the cave, behind the boulder towards the mysterious exit. Striding down a short tunnel, he turned a corner that opened up into a second, smaller cavern. This one, however, was made for man. Brackets holding flame-filled torches lined the walls, a simple kitchen took up one corner, and a four-poster bed took up another. She gasped and glowered at him accusingly.

Arius laughed. "Yes, yes, I should have shared this with you sooner. In my defence, I deemed you to be my prisoner for the first few days. I know things... changed between us, and I should have shown you then. But I didn't trust myself not to lose my heart. Trouble is, I've been dishonest with myself." He gazed deeply into her eyes before uttering, "I already have."

Her heart stuttered. "What? What do you mean?"

He gently placed her down and tucked her hair back from her face. "I love you, Seraphina."

"But... you're a dragon. You can't love... a human." She changed the word from 'me' at the last second.

"I am also a man. Trust me when I say I have wrestled with the shame of sullying my family's name with our pairing—"

Her insecurities reared up and she lashed out at the insinuation she wasn't good enough, snapping, "I'm sorry if I don't meet your standards. It's not like I can just grow wings and a tail." She had intended for the words to be clever and biting but they sounded hollow when spoken aloud.

He gave her a placating smile. "I meant no offence. The reality is, a human and dragon together, even one that can shift, well, it's considered aberrant by my kind. And I assume the humans wouldn't exactly be thrilled by it?"

Keeping her gaze cast down, she nodded. "I would be called perverted and most likely locked up in the IRC."

"And yet..." He cupped her face in his hands and leaned his forehead against hers. "I will renounce my nature if that's what it takes. You are everything I have ever wanted, and never knew I needed. I don't care what the others say. I need you. I love you. Please, tell me I am not alone in this?"

Overwhelmed, Sera broke away and tried to brush past him. Arius grabbed her arm and spun her to face him. "Admit it," he growled, "You love me."

"That's ludicrous!" she exclaimed, not meeting his penetrating stare, and struggled to extract herself from his grip.

"Then why won't you look at me?" he challenged her with a raised eyebrow.

She defiantly raised her eyes to prove to him that he had no claim on her, but as soon as they locked eyes, she couldn't summon the strength to pull away. He grasped her waist with his left hand and drew her closer while his right hand wound itself in her hair. He tilted her jaw up, his face so close, his lips hovering in front of hers. He stopped in this position, waiting for her to close the last few centimetres between them. She gazed into his eyes and saw a question lurking in their green depths. Would she give herself to him? Arius was leaving the final choice up to her. She could disentangle herself now and walk away from this affair, or she could give everything to him. If she gave in, it wouldn't just be her body; she knew her heart would belong to him too. There would be consequences if anyone ever found out, she knew that. They teetered on the brink of the forbidden abyss. He waited, as still as if he were carved from stone. Sera hesitated, her mind a jumble of thoughts about what was the right thing to do by society, and what was the right thing to do by her heart. A sigh escaped as she released what little control she had left and touched her lips to his. As they finally connected, a feeling like fire raced across her skin, taking hold of any remnants of uncertainty in her mind and burning them away. She groaned as he crushed his body against hers, his kiss searing her lips, claiming her.

CHAPTER TWENTY-FOUR

HER HEART HAMMERED INSIDE her chest and her emotions threatened to consume her. Trembling, she ran her hands over his body, feeling the tense muscles ripple under her fingertips. A tremor shook his body and she tore herself away to appraise him.

"You're shaking?" she asked him, perplexed.

Breathing heavily, a half-smile quirked his lips up. "This is new for me too."

"You mean, you've never...?" She blushed, unable to finish the sentence.

"No. Not in my human form. It's a... a foreign feeling. It's a deeper, more spiritual connection in dragon form. This is... very physically intense." He smiled at her and softly brushed his lips against her cheek.

A craving bloomed inside her, and all she wanted was to be touched by him, all over her body, for the rest of her life. The carnal desires were suddenly overtaken by another feeling. A strange and powerful surge of electricity swept through her body, making her ache. Her skin was too tight, and she was feverish. She felt as if her very soul had ignited. The same pain was echoed on his face.

"What is this?" she whispered, her blood on fire.

Grimacing, he rasped, "I think... I think you're my Soulbound. We have to complete the sacred rite. Now."

A small part of her brain yelled that before they committed to doing anything she needed to know what a Soulbound was, and why her insides were burning. But the increasing agony of her boiling body shut out all logic and demanded a release from this pain in whatever form it took.

"How?" she gritted out between her teeth.

"Let me show you."

Arius held his hand up and allowed his nail to elongate into a dragon talon. Taking his claw, he drew a line diagonally across his chest, over his heart. Blood welled up and dripped down his muscles. He took her trembling hand and cut a line along the palm, then placed it over his wound. She gasped. His blood sought a way into her body, and as it entered her bloodstream the crackling heat that had threatened to burn away her senses cooled. Amazed, she looked at him. His face was still tormented.

"Sorry," he ground out, before yanking her shirt out of the way and raking his talon over her heart.

She hissed at the sting as blood trickled over her breasts. His hand shook as he tore a jagged line across his own palm and pressed it to her heart. He moaned as her blood seeped into his veins. The distress melted away, leaving his features clear and relaxed. Their souls sang as they bled into each other, their life force combining. The bleeding slowed until the lacerations grew warm and sealed, both beings healed and whole. Panting, they stayed melded together, hands to hearts, for a long time.

Eventually, she reluctantly broke their connection. "So, tell me. What exactly is a Soulbound?"

He muttered to himself, "How to explain it so you can understand..." He glanced at her upturned face and softly kissed her nose. "It is a sacred rite as old as the Four Gods themselves. I suppose the easiest way for you to understand, is that it's similar to the human's concept of true love. Our souls are bound to one another for life. It is a rare enough event among my kind. I've never heard of a dragon and a human soulbinding before," he pondered, his gaze distant.

She rubbed the dried blood off her body and noticed a faint golden scar where he had cut her. Studying the lines, she commented, "Before we... became Soulbound, it felt like my blood was on fire. Did you feel the same thing?"

"Yes. That is the final confirmation of the Gods' will."

"Are you serious?" She raised an eyebrow.

"The Four Gods are as real as you and me, Seraphina. I will teach you more of their history one day."

"Okay. Let's just assume for the moment that I am accepting the Gods' existence as real and that they actually care about us mere mortals. Are you telling me, that no matter what I did in my life, I was going to end up bound to you because that was the will of the Gods?" Disturbed, she combed her fingers through her hair in agitation.

"No. No single being's destiny is written in stone. The future is always fluid. A series of choices made by you is what led you to me. A series of choices made by me is what led me to you." He smiled but it didn't reach his eyes. Doubt and fear clouded his expression.

Sera caressed his face. "I'm pretty sure what I'm about to say is coming from me and not the Gods, Arius. I love you. I think a part of me loved you from the very first time I saw you."

He buried his face into her neck, strands of her auburn hair mingling into his chocolate. "You said the words." His shoulders raised as he took a steadying breath. "You said you loved me."

He raised his head to gaze at her, his eyes shining. Sera leant forward and tenderly kissed him. He moaned and drew away to stroke her cheek softly with his thumb, his eyes following the motion. Arius tilted his head and kissed her jawline, slowly moving down her neck, tracing a line of fire along her collarbone.

He leant his forehead against hers and closed his eyes. She inhaled his heady scent while her heart beat loudly in her ears. Suddenly, she was looking at herself through his eyes. Seeing her tangled locks woven through his fingers, feeling her pulse beat wildly against his lips, tasting the perspiration on her skin. Her eyes were closed in ecstasy from his tender ministrations. Releasing her internal tension, she easily returned to her own body, opened her eyes and pulled away.

"I need some time to come to terms with everything that's happened." She smiled ruefully, her wanton desires battling against her reasoning.

His bright emerald eyes dimmed, but he nodded as he broke his contact with her. "I can respect that."

They sat down on the bed, careful not to touch one another for fear of sparking the agonising attraction again. Picking at a loose thread on her ripped shirt, she asked, "What happens if a dragon's Soulbound dies?"

"The binding is broken. It almost destroys the dragon that is left behind. It crushes their soul and turns them into a shadow of their former self. I've heard of some who would seek out an early death. They used to find a Hunter who would kill them, but now that the humans believe we're extinct, they have to find more creative ways to die. There is the occasional dragon who survives the breaking of the bond and utilises their talents to serve the dragon society. Like my father."

"Your father was Soulbound to your mother?"

"Yes. When she died, it nearly killed him. Maybe that's why he has such a jaded view of the world." He sat still, lost deep in thought for a time. Shaking himself out of his reverie, he met her gaze once more and smiled as he said, "I don't know about you, but I'm famished."

Sera laughed at such a normal remark, her amusement echoing around the room. The darkness stole into the cave, signalling the late hour. The flames from the torches threw patterns of light across their faces as they ate dinner together, Arius remaining in human form.

Pausing mid-meal, she asked him, "What happened after I passed out on the plateau?"

A look of consternation crossed his face. "Desamor was all for killing you while you were unconscious, but my father put a stop to that. He allowed me to fly you back here and said we would meet tomorrow morning to discuss your future. I think Aliah was hoping to sway him towards leniency." He sighed. "I suppose we'll just have to wait and see."

Finishing his meal, he folded his hands behind his head and asked, "Would you care to share my bed tonight? I'm not asking for anything more than that. I would just like to be close to you and for you to be comfortable."

He watched her closely, gauging her reaction. Her heart faltered at the idea of his body lying against hers. Her cheeks flushed, and she berated herself for her bashfulness.

Don't be coy. You just shared your blood with each other. Your souls are bound together in some weird God-approved dragony way. Pretty sure you'll have to get used to touching him.

Aloud she queried, "I thought you struggled to maintain human form for long without sapping your energy."

"It's strange," he replied. "After the binding, I feel… stronger, somehow. I would like to try to sleep beside you. If I can't maintain this form, I'll just transform back and sleep out there." He nodded towards the outer cave. Pausing uneasily, Arius fidgeted before saying, "I'm just so afraid of what tomorrow will bring. I want to share one night of peace with you if I can."

Casting her fears aside, she whispered, "I would like that."

CHAPTER TWENTY-FIVE

THE FEEL OF HIS lean body enfolding hers through the night on the mattress had delivered her the best night's sleep she'd had in over a week. Upon waking from her deep slumber, Sera found the bed empty and cold. Her heart ached from the dragon-shaped hole that had been carved into it. Disorientated, and unsure if it was daylight yet, she stumbled from the dark room and blindly followed the tunnel to the main cave. There she found Arius cooking breakfast over the fire in human form. Relieved, she ran to him and threw her arms around him.

"Good morning," he murmured into her hair as he returned her embrace. "I trust you slept well?"

"Amazingly." She grinned at him, unbridled joy making her chest feel like it was too small to hold so much emotion.

The weak sunlight filtering through the clouds was unexpectedly blotted out by a dark shape that filled the cave entrance. Desamor's body landed heavily on the rocky floor, his claws grating against the stone. Arius let go of her and moved forward. As she watched, his body writhed and he fell onto all fours as wings burst from his back, spikes erupted along his spine and scales covered his body.

His massive dragon form erupted forth and he bared his teeth in warning at his brother. "Why are you here, Desamor?"

Desamor snorted. "I've come to make sure the human hasn't decided to sneak off. I don't trust you to obey our father's orders."

"As you can see, she is still here, as per his request. You can leave now. You are not welcome in my home."

Desamor raised his snout, flaring his nostrils. "Some home. It even smells like—" he stopped mid-sentence as he sniffed the air and his pupils dilated. "You have bound your soul to her?" he hissed. "Traitor! Defiler! Worm!" He roared his fury. "How dare you dilute the sacred blood of our mother. You desecrate the name of our family. Indeed, you violate the very word dragon. You will die for this! But you will see your little pet be ripped apart first!"

He lunged toward her.

Arius met him head-on and the crash of their two bodies colliding sent a shockwave running through Sera's body. The sound echoed through the cavern, reverberating off the rocks. She watched in horror as the black dragon sunk his claws into the coppery shoulder of Arius and gnashed his teeth at his wings. The thin membranes had never seemed so delicate. In retaliation, Arius raked his talons along Desamor's underbelly, trying to hook a claw around one of the plates while his jaws tried to break through the obsidian armour. It looked an even fight; both dragons were of a similar size, although the older brother appeared more muscular. Arius may not have the bulk behind him, but he was nimble. They broke apart and both uttered a battle cry. The explosion of sound within the confined space left Sera deafened and reeling. She fell to the floor, hands clasped to her ears, and waited for her equilibrium to return before struggling to her feet once more. A blast of flame hit a stalagmite beside her and singed her hair. The rock formation melted like wax under the intense heat. In her shock from the turn of events, she felt detached from the clash of the two dragons and observed the changes curiously.

So this is how the stalagmites were so smooth in my cage. Who knew a dragon's fire melted stone?

A black wing struck a stalactite above Sera's head and she snapped back into focus as she bolted away to avoid the falling structure. Chips of stone struck her back, slicing through her skin. Arius swung his head toward her, desperate to ensure her safety, and Desamor took advantage of his exposed neck. Charging forward he bit down on his jugular.

"No!" Sera screamed and whipped out Firinne, unsure if the short blade would pierce Desamor's hide, but willing to try if it meant saving her dragon.

"Run!" Arius yelled at her before his words cut off into a gurgle as his brother's jaw tightened around his throat. Rivulets of blood trickled down his neck, staining his scales a bright red.

"I won't leave you!" she yelled as she sprinted towards the two writhing forms.

"You must!" He swung his wing like a club into Desamor's head to loosen his hold before sweeping his tail towards Sera to halt her dash.

Sobbing, she leapt out of the way of the swinging tail and landed in the stream that ran through the cavern. The surprise of the freezing mountain water made her pause. Logic seeped back into her brain. Her dragon would be more likely to get hurt trying to save her than if he could give his full focus to the combat. Turning away, she raced towards the dark hole in the wall from where the creek sprang. Arius managed to twist away and give a powerful beat of his wings, throwing dust up into the other dragon's eyes, allowing Sera to scramble into the tunnel, away from the fatal teeth of Desamor.

Hunched over to avoid scraping her head on the low roof of the passage, Sera followed the stream. The awkward position she held herself in wasn't helped by the darkness, and she kept catching her shoulders on the sides of the channel. The water flowed just below her knees, the dampness spreading up her trousers as she splashed onward. Every time she tripped over a hidden rock and caught herself, she felt the grazes on her hands deepening. She focused on the sting of the fresh injuries in the hopes that it would stop her worrying about what was happening back in the cave.

I couldn't bear it if something happened to him because of me. Think, Sera, think! She had to figure out a way to help Arius. She refused to consider what might happen to her if he died in battle. *But what could I do? I'm stuck in this tunnel right now, with no idea of who is winning.* At least she knew he was still alive as their deafening roars reverberated through the stone.

She kept moving forward, away from the sound of the dragon fight. Crashes still echoed through the space that seemed to shake the very foundations of the mountain. Sera was petrified that the natural corridor might collapse on her head. At that thought, she felt a tightness in her chest, and her breathing came in short, sharp pants. A faint blue light glowed up ahead, so she followed it, scrabbling desperately up the incline as the passage narrowed, adding to her claustrophobia.

Heaving herself through a tight spot, she burst out onto a dimly lit ledge. Her mouth dropped open as she drank in the sight before her. The shelf she was perched on was a few metres above the floor of a grotto that was mostly taken up by a clear pool. Bioluminescent fungi decorated the walls, their flat caps emitting the pale glow, while thin roots snaked down the walls. She assumed this was the spring that fed the stream but gaped in bewilderment as she observed the direction of the current.

It's flowing UP! That's impossible!

As it left the spring, the water climbed the wall below her and rushed up and over onto her ledge. She shook her head, astounded. Her skin prickled, the magic that filled this cavern palpable. Sera's eyes were drawn inexorably down into the depths of the pool. Leaning further out she noticed a strange shimmer at the bottom. Carefully, so as not to disturb any of the glowing mushrooms, she swung her legs over the edge, turned so she faced the wall and lowered her body down. She hung from the rocky outcrop for a moment, glanced down to check her trajectory, then let go.

CHAPTER TWENTY-SIX

BENDING AT THE KNEES, she allowed her hips to absorb the impact of her landing. Straightening slowly, she cautiously approached the abnormally still pool. She flinched as a massive boom rocked the ground. Small fragments fell from the grotto's roof and split the perfect reflection in the water, creating multiple fractured images of herself standing in front of the glowing fungi. The images warped and shifted into the likeness of another woman. Dropping forward on to her hands and knees, she peered at the vision in the water that was both the same and different from her. The figure in her reflection did not mimic her movement.

Sera stiffened, eyes darting over the woman in front of her, trying to make sense of what she was seeing. The image was ethereal. She hesitantly touched the surface of the water only for her hand to pass through the woman. Ripples distorted the vision for a moment, and when they stilled the woman's face zoomed into focus. Sera froze, mouth agape, as she recognised the face. It was her mother.

Elisabeth. The woman who had birthed her, who had willed her knife be gifted to her at graduation, who had died and left her and her father alone when she was just a babe.

How is she here? What is this place? "Mum." A whisper was all Sera could muster.

The version of Elisabeth in the pool didn't react to her words and turned her face to the side and murmured to someone. Sera gasped as revelation struck. This was a Seeing Pool. They were incredibly rare. She had never seen one in person before and had only read about them in class at MINATH. They were said to offer insights into the past and prophesies of the future. Eagerly, she leant forward and listened closely to her mother's words, desperate to hear the voice she hadn't heard for twenty-one years.

"Darling, I must speak with you." Elisabeth's eyes were tight as she spoke softly to the shadowy figure at the edge of the pool.

"What is it, my beloved?" a male's voice responded.

Sera frowned. *That's not Dad's voice.*

"I have Seen a prophecy of the future. Of our future."

A sharp intake of breath was all that greeted her words.

"We will have a child together. It will be a girl..." Sera's mother lowered her eyes to her clenched hands and took a shaky breath.

"That is our deepest wish, my beloved. Why do you seem unhappy?" he asked gently.

"Her name will be Seraphina."

A knot coiled in Sera's stomach. *This can't be right. My father is Allen. And this is not his voice.*

"It doesn't have to be," came the snarled reply. "You've said yourself, these visions are not set in stone. We can choose another name."

"That's true. But there was something about this one..."

"I will not allow you to name our daughter after a damned dragon!"

"I'm just telling you what I saw." Elisabeth smoothed her ginger hair back into a bun, the hairstyle severe. "There's something else."

"Out with it then," came the curt response.

"She will change everything. She will save us all from a path of destruction. But... if she's told about her true heritage, she will die and all will be lost."

"What do you mean, her true heritage? Are you saying she can't know that we're her parents?"

Elisabeth paused briefly before she said, "Something like that, yes."

Sera sat in shock at the prediction. *Could it be true?*

Elisabeth touched the blade that hung at her side and rubbed the staghorn handle. She recognised Firinne now, although it felt strange to see her knife at someone else's hip, even if it was her mother's. Sera cocked her head as she studied her. If she was anything like her daughter, that subtle habit suggested she wasn't telling the whole truth.

What is she hiding?

The blurred figure off to the side moved forward, closer to her mother. Sera strained her eyes, desperate to see who this man was.

"Well, Eli, we'll just have to be careful not to fall pregnant until we understand this prophecy a little better." The man's voice was a caress now, the earlier aggression carefully hidden. Sera didn't trust him.

Her mother reached a hand toward him as she said, "I know, Mal."

Mal? Who in the Four Gods' names is Mal?

His face would be revealed at any moment as they moved toward each other in the vision, each step bringing his features further into focus. Until an explosion rent the air and a rock crashed down into the pool, shattering the image. Cringing away from the splash, Sera tore her eyes away and stared horrified at the broken ledge behind her. Dust billowed out of the tunnel as the ceiling cracked. The dragon's battle had caused a cave in. There was no way out.

CHAPTER
TWENTY-SEVEN

BOUNDING AWAY FROM THE falling debris, utter panic clouded her mind. Fear closed its grip on her soul, crushing her lungs with its force.

I'm going to die here.

The tightness in her chest made breathing a challenge. The grotto rocked again with another boom and more chunks of the ceiling splashed into the pool. Wayward shards grazed her body as the boulders ricocheted off the walls. Amidst the destruction, Sera's instincts took over, reverting to the Tracker training that was as much a part of her as Firinne was. She concentrated on slowing her racing heart as she tuned out the chaos surrounding her.

I need to find a way out. There's always more than one option. I can't just stay here and wait to be buried alive.

On a whim, she cast her mind out. She noted the nearby auras of tiny insects that lived in the mountain, scurrying away from the commotion. She sensed the two dragons grappling together back in the cave. Pulling back closer to herself, she grasped a vague sense of sentient life dotting the walls around her. Frowning, she trained her focus on the fragile auras and realised it was the fungi. They whispered to her in a strange language. While she couldn't understand their words, Sera received an impression of cold darkness and narrow spaces. Confused, she glanced around the cavern, trying to see if there was another exit that she'd missed in her first assessment.

As her eyes swept the room, one of the glowing mushrooms gleamed brighter. As soon as her eyes landed on it, its light dimmed and the one below it shone out. When her eyes moved to the new light, it too dimmed and the one below it lit. This continued as her eyes followed the light trail that disappeared into the Seeing Pool. Others lit up underwater, their glow illuminating a submerged tunnel that until then had been shrouded in the darkness.

Not my favourite idea of escape, but better than waiting here to be crushed by the mountain.

Taking a deep breath, Sera gritted her teeth and dived into the freezing water.

Mushrooms lit her path as she swam away from the ruined grotto. Rock enclosed her on all sides, and she felt the tightness in her chest again as the already narrow space seemed to shrink around her. She kept holding her breath and used her arms to pull her body through the space and her legs to kick her forward.

I hope the mushrooms know I need to breathe soon. A dreadful idea consumed her thoughts. *What if I escaped being killed by the cave-in, only to drown in this tunnel?* The knowledge that she could die in here when she ran out of oxygen just made her more determined to escape. *I refuse to let my fear defeat me. If I die, I need to know I did everything I possibly could to save myself.*

The tunnel tapered even further, and her hips stuck between the walls. The feeling of constriction filled her with dread but she wriggled from side to side, peeling skin from her body with every movement. Her lungs were burning. With a violent kick, she squeezed through the narrow passage and shot out the other side. The blue light of the mushrooms shone a trail that led upwards.

Hope bloomed in her chest as she pushed all her remaining energy into powerful strokes, ignoring the flare of pain in her hips as she followed the glow. With one last kick, she broke free of the water and rattled in a lungful of air. Wheezing, she pulled herself out of the water and flopped onto the floor of another small cavern. Rolling onto her back, she rested her hand against the wall and gently stroked the top of the nearest mushroom.

"Thank you," she whispered.

A tendril hanging from the mushroom wound around her finger for a moment and squeezed as if in reaction to her words before releasing her. As she lay there catching her breath, she realised the blue glimmer of the fungi wasn't the only light in this place. Tilting her head, she spotted a soft greenish-grey glow above her. Carefully, Sera turned onto her side and pushed herself up into a sitting position.

It's the sky!

She could have wept in relief. Instead, she hauled herself onto her feet, using the wall for support. The gloomy daylight was just visible through a curtain of vines that hung down the cliff face. Steeling herself, Sera scaled the side of the small cave, using the cracked and uneven wall for foot and handholds. It was only a short climb, but it taxed the last reserves of her strength. She made it to the opening and found a ledge that jutted out from the mountainside to pull herself onto. Puffing, she gathered herself before pushing the vines aside and poking her head through the hole.

I've never been so happy to see the sky. Closing her eyes, she lay on the outcrop and basked for a moment in the fresh air.

A roar to her left made her snap her eyes open. She gasped in horror as the black and copper scales of the two dragons mingled into a bizarre version of a yin-yang symbol as they tumbled out of the cave entrance and into the air. They grappled together, battling for the upper hand. They continued to free fall and Sera covered her mouth with a hand, a whimper escaping as she imagined Arius' body smashing to the earth. That thought must have also been in the dragon's minds as they pulled apart before they came too close to the ground. Arius spread his wings and pushed himself away from Desamor with his talons. The wind filled them like sails and broke his fall, but his wing beats seemed laboured as he soared away from Desamor.

"Arius!" she yelled, but she was too far away for him to hear. *If only I could help him.*

She glanced above her head and grabbed a vine. She gave it a hard tug, thinking she could use it as a rope to climb or swing to safety. The roots let go and the vine fell into a coil at her feet.

No luck.

She glared at the vine. She tried others, all with the same result. She was fairly certain the vine itself was sturdy enough to take her weight without breaking, but the root system didn't have enough of a grip on the cliff to hold her.

So, I survived a cave-in and almost drowning, only to get stuck on the side of a cliff. If only I had wings of my own.

With that thought, her head snapped up and located Arius. He barrel-rolled through the sky, avoiding Desamor's outstretched talons. Sinking into the semi-meditative state that was becoming second nature to her now, she called his name inside his mind. He pivoted mid-air and his emerald eyes found her. He let out a relieved bellow. Swiftly switching direction, he surprised Desamor by using his tail spikes to tear a hole in the membrane of the black dragon's wing. A pained snarl tore from his maw as he struggled to right himself using his injured limb. Her dragon came hurtling toward her, and as he closed the distance between them she noticed red streaks of blood that stained his scales. She bit her lip to hold back a sob.

Are you okay, Arius?

I could ask you the same, Sera. I'm going to have to try to land underneath you and hold onto the cliff face with my talons. You will have to jump on my neck. Do you think you can do that?

Fear flooded her but she tamped it down. This wasn't much different to some of the training scenarios she'd completed as a Tracker at MINATH. Albeit without the part where she jumped on to a dragon's back and all that stood between her and certain death was the empty sky.

Yes. I can. She grabbed one of the vines at her feet in case she needed it and tied it around her waist. *I'm ready.*

You will have to be quick. Desamor's injury won't slow him down for long and he'll be on us sooner than you think.

Sera withdrew from his mind. Arius closed in on her perch, slowing his beating wings and tilting his body so he would land feet first against the cliff face just below her. She grimaced as he hit hard and dug his claws in, sliding a little as they gained purchase. Letting her instincts take over, she lined up the jump and refused to think about the consequences of failing. Out of the corner of her eye, she noted the dark shape of their adversary winging towards them. Setting her mouth in a grim line, she leapt.

CHAPTER TWENTY-EIGHT

THERE WAS A MOMENT of suspension as she took the leap of faith before she felt her stomach in her mouth as she dropped sickeningly through the air. Sooner than she expected, she smacked into his neck. The scales were slick with blood and she scrabbled frantically to stop her fall. Snatching at the closest neck spine, she managed to hang on. A black shadow blotted out what little sunlight there was as Arius pushed off from the mountainside, wings folded close to his sides, and dropped straight down.

"Goddess, damn it!" Sera swore as her tentative hold slipped.

Desamor's great shape smashed into the cliff where they had just been hanging and he screeched his fury at missing his prey. Arius spread his wings and levelled himself out, allowing her time to crawl along his neck to her usual seat at the base of his neck.

"Sorry about that." He flung the words over his shoulder, shouting to be heard over the wind. "Are you all right?"

Yeah, I'm okay, she answered in his mind. *Exhausted. But unharmed.*

Let me try something. You might want to hold on tightly in case it doesn't work.

Gripping the spine in front of her, fatigue seeped into her bones. She had already pushed herself to the limit in the cave, and now they were being chased by a dragon intent on both of their deaths. Her thoughts were interrupted by a strange electricity that crackled through her senses. The shock wasn't unpleasant, though. The current shot through her blood and a jolt of energy engulfed her. Invigorated, she grasped the spine tighter as Arius wobbled mid-air.

What was that? she asked him, straightening up.

The bond. I have been told that Soulbounds can share their life force with one another. I wasn't sure if I could do it. Not the ideal scenario to practise in, but desperate times...

Are you okay, though? You shouldn't have risked yourself on my account.

I'm fine. I can't live without you so I will always risk myself before allowing you into danger.

That's sweet, but I can take care of myself. So, what's the plan then?

Arius didn't answer immediately, just flew as fast as his damaged wings would allow him. *Honestly... I don't know. I need to get you to safety. I don't want to kill my brother, but he's after our blood. I'm not sure if I'll have another option.*

Sera mused on their predicament as the wind howled past her ears and the ominous form of Desamor gained on them.

Desamor won't drop this feud until I'm dead. If he kills you in his pursuit of me, she shuddered at the thought, *I'm as good as gone. I don't think Desamor will be waiting around to see what your father decides. If you kill him, I might be safe for a little while longer, but I have no idea what your father will do to us. There must be another option.*

Her father's voice echoed in her mind. "There's always another way, darling girl." It was his favourite saying. She smiled as a plan started to take shape.

Arius, I have an idea. I will need you to trust me. And to catch me if I fall.

What are you going to do? He twisted his head so he could eyeball her.

I don't think you'll like it. So, all I need you to know is that I need you to fly above Desamor.

Arius raised an eyebrow and gave a disgruntled snort. *Fine. Hold on tight.*

Sera lost her stomach once again as he angled his head up and fiercely beat his wings, shooting straight up through the cloud cover. They glided on silent wings, and Sera gazed around in wonder at the silver dusted clouds; they could have been flying over a steely ocean. She wished she could stop and take in the moment, but for her plan to work they would need the element of surprise. Arius adjusted his wings and lowered them deeper into the blanket of cloud cover.

Sera took a moment to get her bearings as her vision turned grey, the beads of water sliding off the spines in front of her, making the ivory bones slick. The wind still whipped past her, grasping at her clothes and threatening to pull her from his back. Bending at the waist, she ducked her head low and leaned over the side of Arius' neck as far as she dared. She heard a frustrated snarl from somewhere below as Desamor searched the skies for them.

I need us to go lower.

I don't like this, came his taut reply.

You don't have to like it. You just have to trust me.

She withdrew from his mind. She'd need all her wits about her to win this battle. Arius descended further, careful to keep them hidden in the clouds. A second set of wingbeats came into earshot, and Sera checked that the vine was still wrapped around her waist, before pulling Firinne out of its sheath.

"Here goes nothing," she whispered to herself.

She drew her knees up and settled into a crouch, using the nearest spine to balance. Peering down, she could just make out the dark form of Desamor visible through the mist, only a few metres below and slightly behind them. He saw them at the same time and released a triumphant roar at detecting his quarry. With that, she let go and dropped through the air.

The wind pushed against her, threatening to send her off course and plummeting to her death. Tightening her core, she kept her eyes locked on the black dragon and spread her arms and legs out to slow her freefall. His eyes widened in shock as she fell towards his neck, landing hard; the air left her lungs in a whoosh. Ignoring the pain, she dug her blade into Desamor's neck as she started to slide and used her momentum to swing up onto his back. Moving quickly before he had time to fully comprehend what was happening, Sera settled into a gap between two spines. She used the vine from her waist to fasten herself against the spike at her back to make it difficult for him to throw her off and tightened the cord just in time. Scales rumbled beneath her as he released a torrent of fiery rage. Screeching, he launched himself into a series of complicated aerial manoeuvres in an attempt to dislodge her. Doing her best to ignore the acrobatics, she closed her eyes and placed her hands against his scales.

Feral aggression met her when she entered Desamor's mind. A mental wall of power slammed into her, leaving her gasping. She thought of the way she had gotten around Talegar's defences and concentrated on making her spirit as ethereal as the wind that still lashed her physical body. Her mind leant into the wall that Desamor had thrown up, applying pressure until it crumbled to dust beneath her.

White-hot rage filled him and made her feel as if her soul were on fire.

Stop this! She shouted the words into his mind.

Never! He was incensed at her presence, and she got the feeling that nothing she said would change his opinion of her.

I don't want to hurt you. Please, let's talk.

He roared his opposition, refusing to consider her request.

You leave me no choice. I'm sorry.

Not wasting any time looking at his chaotic memories, Sera propelled herself through the turbulent seas of his mind. Ignoring the sticky, black tendrils of thought that spread towards her, she quickly located the glowing doorway that led to the next level. The light was different from Arius'. It gave off a sickly green glow and she had to shove her way through. A little part of her questioned the morality of her actions, worried that she would damage his brain irreparably. She waved the thought away. It came down to survival. If she wanted to live another day and save Arius, she couldn't afford the luxury of mercy.

As she sunk into the second level, Desamor focused on attacking her within his mind. In doing so, his wings faltered and they dipped closer to the ground. He roared in frustration and beat his wings violently to avoid crashing. She felt his pain as the wind tore at the damaged membrane. The warmth was building in his chest again as he longed to spew fire onto her body, his thoughts screaming for her to get out. As they rose into the air again, Sera did what Talegar had asked of her. She forced her way into the third level.

She sensed Desamor's shock and fury as if it were her own as she violated his mind. She gathered the glimmering green lines that controlled his body and on instinct clumsily heaved on them. His wings flared open, and his body swung perpendicular to the ground, slowing their forward motion. She kept pulling the strings and forced him to turn back towards the plateau. She could see Talegar and Aliah standing on the cliff's edge, watching the battle unfold. She compelled him to fly back to them, keeping a tight grip on the reins of his mind. A distant screeching vainly beat at the back of her mind, but she brushed it off easily. The absolute supremacy she felt as she manoeuvred the massive body of the largest predator in the world was indescribable. And it terrified her.

CHAPTER
TWENTY-NINE

ALIAH OPENLY GAWKED AS Sera guided the black dragon's body awkwardly onto the plateau. Talegar's gaze
remained guarded as they landed heavily in a billow of
dust. She opened their mouth and forced Desamor to
speak her words.

"I have done as you asked, Talegar. I have controlled
your son. But I only did this to save Arius and myself."
Though the words were her own, they sounded strange
in his voice. "I swear to the Four Gods I will not use this
power for evil."

Talegar snorted at her words. "Surely you have learnt
by now? There is no good and evil. There are facets of
light and dark in all things."

He watched shrewdly as his youngest son landed in a
hurried heap in front of them. Arius snaked his head back
and forth as he tried to comprehend what was happening.

Talegar continued with an impatient toss of his head,
"Sometimes you have to do evil things for good reasons."

She opened her mouth to argue but bit back her retort
when she recognised that she had just done precisely
that. In her effort to save the life of Arius she had taken
away the free will of Desamor, manipulating him as if he
were no more than a puppet. Feeling sick, she withdrew

her iron grip on his mind. All was quiet in the once-turbulent ocean of his thoughts as she extracted herself. Coming back to her own body, she sucked in a gasp of air. It felt like her lungs were no longer large enough to hold the amount of oxygen she needed. She shook herself free of the last vestiges of the dragon's aura. With trembling fingers, she untied the vine that had kept her human body from plunging to the earth. The usual dizziness that accompanied her exit from a dragon's mind didn't hit, instead, a familiar hum of electricity trickled through her veins. Her brows knitted as she looked up to meet Arius' apprehensive gaze.

You're feeding me energy again?

Yes. Relief coloured his tone.

Once again, thank you. I wouldn't have been able to do that without your help. But you shouldn't keep giving me energy. You're hurt! She winced as she noticed the open slashes on his neck and the blood coating his wings.

I'll be fine. He bowed his head. *It is I should be thanking you. You saved us.* Green fire lit his eyes from within as he drank in her features hungrily. *I am so very relieved that you are safe. Thank the Four Gods.*

She blushed at the depth of his concern for her. Cautiously sliding down the side of the unconscious form of Desamor, she worried her lip as she stepped in front of him.

"What have I done?" She wrapped her arms around her middle, guilt sinking its hooks into her stomach, making her ill. His great body rose and fell with each breath he took, but that was the only sign of life. His eyes remained closed.

"He slumbers, but I believe he will wake before the day is done," came the rumbling response from Talegar. The golden dragon shifted his weight. "I have seen this power once before, but not for many decades." He turned the full weight of his piercing eyes on Sera as if weighing up how much to tell her. "There was another, like you, who could enter the minds of dragons. She could also See."

Aliah's gasp drew Sera's attention. She snaked her head forward, tail twitching in excitement. "Father, do you believe Seraphina is the one spoken of in the prophecy?"

A low warning growl rolled from Talegar's chest. "Do not speak of things you do not understand, Aliah."

A squeak escaped from Aliah as Talegar sent his will crashing into her, cutting off anything further she might have said.

"Prophesy? What prophesy?" Sera darted her eyes over the dragons assembled, trying to decipher what they knew.

Talegar turned back to her as he explained, "There was a prophesy made many years ago, of a human with a dragon's abilities. We always assumed it would manifest in more physical ways, but I suppose there is a chance you could be the one it speaks of. I do not recall the exact wording. We would need to take you to Sky Valley to see if you are the one."

"Sky Valley? Where is that?"

"For the safety of my brethren, I will not reveal the location of our home to a human. I am willing to take you there if you are unconscious for the journey, but I refuse to share the location with you. You are a Tracker at heart, and until I can ensure your loyalty, I will not put all of dragonkind at risk."

"I can understand your concern, but I swear I won't lead anyone to your home."

"You may not have a choice."

"What do you mean?"

"Do you truly believe that your government has the best interests of both humans and mythics at heart?"

"Yes, of course. That's what our entire way of life has been built around since the Mythic War."

A column of smoke drifted from his nostrils as Talegar chortled. "You naïve little thing. Your foolishness would almost be charming if it wasn't so dangerous. What do you think happens in the Iniques Rehabilitation Centre?"

"How do you know about—" She shook her head, deciding to ignore the intimate knowledge the dragons seemed to have about Mandar and the way it operated. "The IRC is committed to serving justice and offering rehabilitation to mythics who have been arrested for unlawful acts," she said, echoing her teachers from MINATH.

"I didn't ask what the IRC claim to do. I asked what you think they do." A dangerous gleam shone in his eyes as he pointed a talon towards her.

"I don't exactly work there. I don't know anything more than what I just said."

"Come now, Seraphina. Arius obviously thinks you're clever enough if he has chosen to risk his life for yours. Use your brain, girl!"

She glanced at Arius in panic and saw he too was locked in place by his father's compulsion.

"I know that not many mythics are rehabilitated into society after going to the IRC. But I assume that is because they've committed crimes against humanity too terrible to give them back their freedom."

"One should never assume anything."

She raised an eyebrow. "You seem to be suggesting that they... what? Kill the mythics just because they can?

What you're insinuating is treason. The whole point of the treaty after the war was to foster peaceful relations!"

Talegar nodded. "It was the point, yes. However, humans do like to dirty their hands in greed and profit. If I were to allow you to return home, your employer will question where you have been for the last week. Assuming that they don't believe any lies you tell them, they will find ways to make you talk. For the safety of Mandar, of course. I am sure they would believe they are doing an evil thing for a good reason, too."

Sera blanched and looked away. His words slithered in her mind like poison, but they had a ring of truth to them. *It can't be true. It's just a conspiracy he's making up to turn me against the MRO.*

Talegar turned his piercing stare away from her disdainfully. "Believe what you want to believe. Eventually, the truth that has been shrouded in darkness will be brought into the light."

"Well... do you at least believe that I bear no ill will towards you and your kind?"

He examined her for a long moment before nodding in assent. "I do believe you are not intending to threaten dragonkind. In fact," he cocked his head slightly, "you may even prove to be useful." He released his magic that had held Arius and Aliah silent and cast a glance at the still-sleeping Desamor. "Regardless, the decision has been made. You will come to Sky Valley where we will determine if you are the one spoken of in the prophecy."

"What if I'm not?" she asked.

"You may still be of some use to me. Consider your life spared."

She sagged with relief. Arius took a step toward his father. "What of Desamor?"

The golden dragon rumbled a low growl. "I will deal with him later. And Arius? You are still exiled. I do not have the authority to lift your banishment."

"WHAT?" he roared and flared his wings wide, tail whipping from side to side in rage. Each word crashed out with a boom as he exclaimed, "You will still take her from me? You cannot. She is my Soulbound!"

Aliah gasped at his revelation and Talegar's eyes widened as he scented the air, tasting the truth of Arius' words.

Sera glanced between them, perplexed by her dragon's sudden rage. She hurried to his side, laid a calming hand on the coppery scales and whispered, "I don't understand."

Aliah raised her voice. "Father, if they're truly Soulbound... that's cruel. Surely you can request a short amnesty from the Elders? Just until we understand Seraphina's role in our future."

He stared down his nose at his son coiled protectively around the woman in front of him, and huffed, "For the sake of the most sacred of bonds, I will appeal to the Elders for a short reprieve. Stay home with your Soulbound, Arius, until I return with their answer." His giant form sprang from the cliff, wings spread wide to catch the air currents, and sailed west.

Arius paced frantically, his talons sinking into the soft ground, snarling his frustration.

"Don't fret, dear brother. It's a better outcome than it might have been."

Arius paused his march and scowled at Aliah. "Seraphina is safe for today, but if the Elders don't grant me amnesty for her trip to Sky Valley, I don't trust father not to sink his fangs into her."

"Arius!" his sister cried out. "Father would never kill her after agreeing to spare her life."

"I didn't mean it literally, sister. There are many ways he could harm her without physically attacking her." Arius tossed a glance at his brother, disgust written on his face.

"I will stay with Desamor until he wakes, brother. You do what you need to do." Aliah gave him a knowing look and gracefully curled up beside the unconscious dragon. Nodding to her youngest brother, she said, "Fly fierce."

He returned her nod and replied, "Strike strong."

Sera moved to her and rested her hand on the opal scales. *Thank you for speaking up to your father for us.* She poured her sincere gratitude through the mental link with Aliah.

The silvery dragon smiled sweetly and nudged her hand. *Love is love. No matter what form it takes.*

CHAPTER THIRTY

THE WIND MADE HER eyes water as Arius flew swiftly to their cave. Upon landing, he shuddered and transformed into a human, before hobbling toward the hidden cavern.

"Wait!" she called, sprinting to overtake him. Grabbing her backpack from the bedroom, she rifled through the contents until she found the container of Heal. "Here, let me help you."

"I'll heal quick enough," came his gruff reply, but he kept his body turned away from her.

Gently, she grasped his shoulder and drew him around to face her. Sucking a hiss through her teeth, she tried not to gag at the ugly wounds that crisscrossed his body. A particularly nasty slash on his neck had only just missed his jugular. Flaps of skin hung uselessly from his chest and his left arm had a massive tear in it, exposing bone. Carefully, she smeared the treatment liberally on his injuries, holding the skin in place and binding them with bandages where she could. Tears pricked her eyes every time he groaned in response to her ministrations.

"Enough," he grunted. "We don't have time for this." He stood quickly and stalked away from her. Refilling her water bottle and collecting some skyberries and jerky from his pantry, he brusquely shoved them in her backpack.

She stood frozen in place in the cave that had so quickly and unexpectedly become home to her, observing his abrupt movements. "What's happening?"

He strode to her and grabbed her face, crushing his lips to hers. Dread stole over his features as he withdrew and caressed her cheek with his thumb. "I have to save you."

"But Talegar said I would be spared, regardless of the Elders' decision about your banishment."

"My father," he spat the words out, "is a master manipulator. Everything he does is to advance his standing. Truthfully, I owe you an apology. When we met, I condemned you and your race, claiming your sole motivation to be greed and power. I had forgotten my father's will to dominate all those who threaten his idea of a perfect world."

Body quivering, he shuddered as he struggled to maintain his human form through the strength of his emotions. "I was banished from the protection of Sky Valley sixty years ago by the Elders. What they didn't know was that I heard them speaking with my father before the trial. He was the one who recommended banishment for my crime." He squeezed his eyes shut as he relived the pain.

"Arius... can I ask? What did you do?"

He looked at her, agony contorting his expression. "It's my fault my mother died." He inhaled a ragged breath. "The Mythic War was raging, and I was only young. It was a chaotic time. I was meant to go on patrol that night, but my mother let me sleep and took my shift. The humans... they shot her out of the air. She is dead because of me." A tear dripped down his cheek.

Sera wrapped her arms around him and leant her head against his chest. His heart thudded loudly against her ear. "That wasn't your fault. Your mother chose to take your shift. The humans were the ones who killed her. How could you be blamed for that?"

"I abandoned my post. Through my actions, a dragon died." Despair lanced across his features again.

"It's up to you to forgive yourself, but the way I see it, you were wrongly convicted. You should have been allowed to grieve with your family, not been thrown out of your home."

He smiled sadly into her hair. "You are so pure." He stroked her back, his mind far away. With a little shake, he pulled away and held her at arm's length. "The point is, the Elders answer to my father now. His going to ask their permission is a farce. He will never let you return home to Mandar and he will never leave us in peace. He will find a way to use our bond as leverage to exploit your power. I don't know what his plan is, but I do believe he wouldn't mind if there was another war between humans and mythics."

Terror gripped her by the throat, making it difficult to breathe. "We can't afford another war," she croaked. "We haven't recovered from the last one yet."

"I know. Neither have the dragons. That's why we can't afford to play along with his game. I have to get you away from here. I can't let him take you to Sky Valley, with or without me. If he takes you there, he wins."

"What should we do?"

"The only place I can think of where you'll be remotely safe is home in Mandar City. At least for now, until we can figure out another plan."

Fresh panic flared as she stared at him. "What about you? I won't leave you."

He ran his fingers through her tresses. "I will take you to the city. I won't be able to stay in human form for days at a time though, so we will meet that obstacle when we come to it."

She pressed her body to his once more and kissed him passionately. The fire from the bond thrummed through her body, leaving her aching and elated in equal measures.

Twining her fingers through his hair she pressed her forehead to his and breathed, "We can do this. Together."

They flew through the night, Arius keeping to the clouds where possible in an attempt to hide his massive form. The heavy comfort of the pack on her back and Firinne in its sheath on her belt made her feel as prepared for this journey as she could. As they skimmed through the intermittent cover, Sera kept looking over her shoulder.

Entering his mind, she voiced her concern. *I think we're being followed.*

Did you see something? Is it Desamor?

She could sense the undercurrent of panic in Arius' voice, his body still recovering from their earlier battle even with the help of Heal. Not to mention the taxing effort of lending his strength to her.

No... it's not a dragon. More human-shaped, but I'm sure I saw wings.

It sounds like it's just a mythic checking to see who is flying through their territory. Hopefully, they will leave us alone.

Shrugging, she dismissed the stranger and focused on the edge of the Red Waste that was fast approaching.

I'll take us as close to the city as I can, then I'll transform and we can walk the rest of the way together, okay?

Sounds like a plan. She rested her body against his, letting the wind stream over her and his steady wingbeats lull her into a dreamlike state.

CHAPTER
THIRTY-ONE

THE TEMPERATURE RAPIDLY DROPPED. Shivering, she opened her eyes and squinted into the dark cloak of night. Heavy, black clouds rolled toward them from the west, travelling far faster than they should. Lightning flickered from within the tempest and thunder mingled with a terrible roar from far away. The unnatural storm sped towards them.

Still linked with Arius, she heard him snarl, *This is Desamor's doing.*

His ire drew her deeper into his consciousness on the raging torrent of his thoughts. Feeling powerless to pull away from his rage, she was sucked into the light in the centre of his mind.

She looked back through his eyes, seeing for the first time the layers of colours that filled the storm. Purples, blues and flashes of green lit up the sky as the lightning crackled through the air. His distress mingled with hers and made it impossible for her to separate their thoughts, forcing her to go to the second level of his mind. She watched her unconscious body lying prone along his neck and winced as it flopped from side to side. The rain and wind had caught up with them and battered Arius. Dread filled her. Her body looked so frail; it would be so easy for it to slip over his side and fall. Sera was acutely aware of her mortality as the storm lashed them. She desperately needed to return to her own consciousness to do what she could to protect herself, but she was paralysed inside his mind. Arius' anxiety heightened her own as the gale ripped at his wings. A blinding bolt of lightning sliced through the air and struck them. The shock jolted her back into her own body. She dragged in a lungful of air before choking on the water that came with it. She frantically swiped the stinging rain from her eyes as she coughed. Blinking furiously, partially blinded by the flash of light, her stomach clenched in fear as Arius' nose dipped toward the earth. His unconscious form began to drop from the sky.

Grasping a spine in front of her, Sera screamed, "Arius! Wake up! You have to wake up!"

She pummelled his scaly hide in the hopes of rousing him. There was no response. Panic set in as they plummeted towards the earth, gravity drawing them inexorably towards certain death. His wings trailed behind them like torn sails, flapping uselessly in the cyclonic winds. His usually powerful body was buffeted by the elements as it cut through the air like a spear.

Unable to see anything through the roiling thunder clouds and painful raindrops, Sera had no idea how close they were to the ground. How close they were to their end. How close she was to losing her dragon. At that moment, she knew in her heart – she would do anything for him. Die for him, if need be. Against all rationale, she truly loved him. Regardless of her own fate, she couldn't bear it if she lost him. With that thought, her mind snapped into focus. If she could take over control of his body, she could save them. Taking a deep breath, she centred herself, ignored the chaos of the storm around her and slipped back inside his mind.

It felt strange to be here without his thoughts surrounding her. The emptiness terrified her. Sera hurriedly moved through his consciousness toward the bright light in the centre. Once in the second level, she sifted through his mind, feeling guilty for intruding and praying he would forgive her, and followed the lines of light that stretched towards his limbs. Unsure if her plan would work while he was unconscious, she gathered up the lines like reins and tugged. His wings snapped open, catching the air and slowing their descent.

Clumsily, she pulled the lines up and down, and his wings corresponded with the movement, albeit jerkily. Guilt wrapped around her heart and squeezed as she took full control of his body. She dispelled her shame with a toss of their head. This was the only way she could save them. She didn't know how to read air currents at all, let alone in a storm, but somehow, she managed to slow their headfirst dive and awkwardly guide him towards the earth. Without warning a bullet of wind slammed into their side. A half-scream, half-roar tore from their throat as Sera's mind snapped back into her own body. She was falling.

She screamed as she rocketed towards the earth, alone in her mind. The darkness of the tempest had swallowed all light, leaving her disoriented. Sera had no idea how close she was to the ground but knew chances of survival were slim. Sooner than she expected, she plunged into the water; they must have been closer to the earth than she thought. Hitting the water was like slamming into a concrete slab. It pressed in on her, crushing her lungs. She strained to make sense of the murkiness that surrounded her. There were bubbles everywhere and she couldn't figure out which way the surface was. Her limbs grew heavy in the freezing lake and her water-logged clothes threatened to drag her into the inky depths. Just as she gave up hope, a thick, sinewy body wrapped around her and pushed her through the water. She screamed in terror and panicked as the last of her oxygen bubbled away from her. Her lungs burned as she struggled to free herself from its coils when her head unexpectedly broke the surface. Coughing and retching, she dragged in the sweet predawn air as the unknown creature released her.

She didn't have to swim far before she crawled up onto the rocky bank as oxygen rattled into her raw lungs. The worst of the storm had passed but light raindrops still smattered the shore. The moon was attempting to peek out from behind the scattered remains of the stormy clouds before it retired over the western horizon. Pulling herself up onto her hands and knees, she expelled the last of the freshwater. Slowly, she rose to her feet and paused to let the world stop spinning. Blearily she scanned the riverbank, following the shadows, trying to locate Arius. Surely, he would have gained consciousness before crashing. Even if he hadn't, the water would have softened his fall and woken him on impact. He would swim to safety as she had.

What if he was still knocked out and has sunk to the bottom? He'll drown.

Anxiety clawed at her gut as minutes ticked by and he didn't appear. Shivering, she began pacing and tried to connect with his mind. Only the easing rain greeted her attempts.

A rustle in the undergrowth at her back made her start and spin around. Her hand automatically grasped Firinne, which, miraculously, was still attached to her hip. Before she could draw the blade from its sheath, a massive beak drew level with her face. She froze. Her eyes followed the sharp lines up to meet the penetrating stare of a strange hippogryph.

"Move!" he commanded as he spread his feathered wings wide, herding her away from the river. She resisted, but the snapping beak that clicked shut beside her ear convinced her to follow his order, for now at least. She cast a last, searching look behind her, before trudging forward, away from the water, and away from her dragon.

CHAPTER THIRTY-TWO

HER GUARD DROVE HER forward relentlessly. She slipped blindly down into a narrow gulley, getting covered in mud, while the hippogryph gave a few beats of his wings to fly over the ditch and easily avoid the sludge. She glowered sullenly at him as he kept her marching away from any chance of finding Arius. She tried to dash away into the cover of night but he struck her with a wing, sending her sprawling into the muck. Her ears rang from the blow. The rain abated as they trudged over a hill together before entering a natural amphitheatre. Hippogryphs lined the sides of the basin and all heads swivelled as one to watch her. Hundreds of pairs of bright golden eyes blinked at her. They all started shrieking in aggressive excitement as they saw her being shepherded to the centre of the bowl, like a virgin about to be sacrificed.

Maybe that's what is happening. After surviving a dragon attack, I'm going to get my throat slit by an overgrown chicken that did it with a horse.

The cacophony of screeching created a wall of sound around her. The stench of oily feathers and manure made her gag. She couldn't think straight. The noise reached such a pitch that she couldn't help but drop to her knees, her hands over her ears. A single, high pitched scream cut through the noise and pierced the night like an arrow.

All the other hippogryphs fell silent, aside from the one who had found her, who hissed, "Bow to our Queen. It is she who will decide your fate."

Their Queen appeared at the top of the hill, staring disdainfully down at the human brought before her. It had to be their monarch; there was no better way to describe this mythic other than regal. She was taller than the rest of her kind and held herself with authority. Her feathers were sleeker and she was the only silver hippogryph there. The others were varying shades of brown and black, their colours seeming lacklustre in comparison. The hippogryphs parted and bowed their heads as their Queen moved through the flock. All aside from one hippogryph that trailed in the Queen's wake, seeming to almost blend into her shadow.

Perhaps it's a bodyguard?

The dim light of the dawning sun fighting to peek through the clouds made it difficult to tell what colour he or she was. The sharp stones on the ground bit into Sera's knees and she made to stand.

The guard cuffed her once more, sending her crashing back to the ground. "Keep your head down, girl. Show our Queen some respect." Stepping forward, he loudly announced, "Your Highness, I found this human at the edge of Lake Eyre."

"What are you doing here, human? Why have you disturbed our nest?" The Queen peered down her beak at Sera.

"I didn't mea—" Sera paused and coughed, trying to clear her raw throat. "I didn't mean to disturb you, Your Highness. I was flying with Arius..." She choked up a little, fighting the anxiety that swirled in the pit of her stomach, wondering if he was alive. "That is to say, I was riding a dragon when the storm hit and we fell into the water back there." She gestured behind her. "If you would let me leave, I will return to the lake, find my dragon, and disturb you no more."

"Dragons don't let humans ride them," the Queen scoffed.

"This dragon, Arius, is my particular friend and has granted me the honour." Sera held back the fact they were Soulbound for now, her instincts telling her it might inflame the tension.

"Even if that is true, dragons don't just fall out of the sky, girl," she sniffed.

"They do when they get struck by lightning," came Sera's sharp retort and she stood up defiantly.

A small hiss from the hippogryph hidden behind the Queen drew her eyes briefly and she frowned. She could just make out the feathery eyebrows that established he was a male, but the Queen's spread wings still hid the rest of his features from her.

"I find that highly unlikely." Turning to the guard who had found her, she asked, "Did you see any sign of a dragon, Atticus?"

"No sign, Your Highness. Although, the human did appear to be searching for someone when I found her."

The Queen surveyed Sera critically, her sharp eagle eyes seeming to penetrate her soul, before stepping aside and snapping, "Torvold! Step forward!" The hippogryph behind the monarch trotted forward, his dappled coat becoming more obvious in the breaking dawn.

It's Tor!

She could have wept with relief as he revealed himself to her. She took a step forward in anticipation but paused when he shot her a warning look.

"It's high time you stepped up, Torvold. You are my son, and the next in line to lead our flock. You need to start taking responsibility and making meaningful decisions, instead of adopting this foolish persona and mocking your heritage." She fluffed her neck feathers up in annoyance before swivelling her head sharply to glare down her beak at Torvold. "You decide this human's fate, now. Do we kill her or let her go? Keep in mind we don't know what her intentions are and we've never trusted a human Tracker before."

The word Tracker was spat out by the Queen with a touch too much venom in Sera's opinion. She sucked a corner of her bottom lip in and glanced over at Tor briefly, making sure to keep her head lowered in respect. She struggled to read his expression; would he honour his mother and her obvious prejudice against humans, or would he try to preserve their new friendship? Tor was utterly still apart from his eyes that stared deep into hers before turning to his mother and Queen.

He sighed and gave his tail a flick. "Mother, I appreciate you allowing me to make this decision. Please know that I would never intentionally put the flock in danger. I shall always endeavour to put family first. Knowing this, I have made my decision. I don't think we should just let her go."

Sera's heart dropped. Tears pricked in the corner of her eyes. She couldn't absorb the fact that not only was her death imminent, but it had been called for by someone she thought of as a friend.

"You only gave me two options," Torvold continued, addressing his mother and the other hippogryphs that were gathered around them, "but there is a third. Not only will I let her go, but I intend to personally help this Tracker, this human, this woman. It is time to stop living in the past and embrace the new age. To move forward, we need to usher in a positive relationship between hippogryph and human. Let us forge an alliance with them! Our race will not survive another century without their help. We are fighting a losing battle against extinction.

"I remember stories of our ten-thousand-strong army fighting alongside the dragons in the Mythic War against the humans seventy years ago. They battled each other for ten years. And look where that's left us. The werewolves hunt us, fewer young are born every year, many have abandoned our nest. We are weak. We are disunited."

He flared his wings wide, his passion plain in his eyes as he walked forward to stand behind Sera, facing his mother.

"Our numbers are few, we have no combat training and the dragons are all but gone. We can't rely on them to save us. We must find new ways to embrace this world, and I believe the best bet we have is to join with Seraphina. She is a friend of the dragons and she is a Tracker at the MRO. She can help us unite the mythic and human world for a better future."

Almost panting from his speech, Tor turned to Sera and swept his wing behind her back, pushing her forward to stand beside him. "She can lead us into the future. I know it. Stand with me. Stand with Seraphina. And make our future one worth fighting for."

Sweeping his wings back, Torvold reared up and loosed a battle cry to the sky. At that moment, she could see him becoming a worthy King of his people. Underneath his cheeky personality, he cared deeply for his flock. He was willing to push boundaries and break tradition to ensure the safety of his kind.

Time stood still. Hundreds of yellow orbs were fixated on the silver hippogryph, waiting for her final edict after hearing her son's passionate speech. Not even the wind dared to disturb the nest.

"Seraphina," the Queen whispered her name, but the word was laden with such animosity it made Sera flinch. "She never told us her name. You know this human already, don't you Torvold? Another one of your little projects." Disappointment dripped from each word as she flung them like daggers at Tor. "You always find a way to destroy my belief in you. I should have known better. You can't be trusted with a decision like this. Your curiosity and endless thirst for knowledge blinds you to the true dangers of the humans." Hurt flickered across the Queen's features briefly as she murmured, "Just like your father."

The last sentence was spoken quietly but Sera discerned the pain it caused Tor. His expression crumpled in sorrow, his beak hanging open in disbelief when the Queen flung her wings wide and announced, "Let it be known! From this day forward, I have no son. Torvold, you are hereby exiled. Leave now and I will let you and the human live. If you ever return, so help me, I will tear you apart myself."

Torvold squeezed his eyes shut briefly, the grief etched plain upon his feathered face. "I'm sorry you feel this way, Mother. I hope one day you can learn to forgive me."

With that, he nudged Sera urgently and presented his back to her. She leapt up and slid her legs around his barrel, just behind his wings. It was strange how quickly she had grown accustomed to flying with Arius. The silky feathers and smooth grey coat she now sat on felt foreign. Her heart twisted as she longed for the comfort of rough scales and familiar warmth. Torvold took a few canter strides before springing into the air, flapping hard, ignoring the wild screeching of his people around him.

CHAPTER THIRTY-THREE

HE FLEW SWIFTLY, FURIOUSLY beating his wings to stay aloft with her added weight and putting as much distance between them and his flock as quickly as possible. They stayed low, skimming the treetops, and made their way westward, aiming for the massive mountain in the distance. The icy wind cut through her wet clothes and bit into her skin. The sun was on their backs now and offered some meagre warmth. The morning light painted everything gold, with no sign of the wicked storm clouds from last night.

"I'm sorry, Torvold," she called out over the wind streaming past them. "This is all my fault."

"Don't be silly, sweetheart. To be honest, it's been a long time coming. My mother and I have never seen eye to eye."

"Still."

Sera worried for him. A terrible grief had passed over his features when his mother announced his banishment. She ran a comforting hand through the feathers in front of her. A low nicker thrummed through his ribs, wordless thanks for her affection and concern.

They landed softly in a clearing a few miles before the start of the Red Waste. She shook her arms and rubbed her numb fingers, encouraging the blood to return to her limbs before dismounting. Concern clouded Tor's face as he turned his head back to her and said, "We've been followed."

Sera spun around and scanned the blue sky, half-expecting to see one of the Queen's guards. A silhouette materialised out of the fluffy clouds before the form of a strange bay hippogryph landed in front of them.

"Bels!" Tor's tone indicated it was a friend of his. He whinnied a greeting. "What are you doing here?"

"Tor," she answered with relief, "I'm sorry. Please forgive me but I had to follow you. Your mother is wrong. I know I shouldn't say that but it's true. You made great points back there, and she let her prejudice cloud her judgement. I will stay with you. I will support you. And you, Seraphina." She nodded her refined head in Sera's direction. "I'm Belisa but everyone calls me Bels. I will do what I can to help."

"It's nice to meet you, Bels. You can call me Sera. Thank you for your concern, but I don't want either of you losing your family because of me." Turning to Tor, she urged him, "Return to your people, Tor. Take Bels home with you. Blame me for swaying your loyalties, if you must. I have to find Arius."

"Didn't you hear my mother?" he asked bitterly. "I'm banished."

"She's your mother! Surely she would allow you back into the fold if you appealed to her?"

"She exiled my father for less. I have been cast out, Sera. Now that Bels has followed me," he turned his sorrowful gaze towards her, "she has also forfeited her right to stay with my mother's flock."

"I'm so sorry," she exclaimed. "Because of me, you have both lost your family."

"We will just have to start one of our own," Bels suggested coyly and grinned boldly at Tor who looked surprised to not be the one flirting for a change.

Feathers ruffled, he turned his back on the female hippogryph and faced Sera. "There will be time to discuss that later. For now, we need to concentrate on finding Arius. You said he fell during the storm?"

She nodded. "He and Desamor got into a fight." She glanced uncertainly at Bels, unsure how much to reveal in her presence. "Afterwards, Arius decided to return me to the safety of my home, but his brother followed us and created that storm. He was hit." She choked up and dashed the tears from her cheeks. Clearing her throat, she continued, "He was hit by lightning, and he – we – fell into the lake." She paused. "Well, I fell into the lake, and I assumed he did too, but I didn't actually see where he landed."

Now that she was free of her fear of the hippogryph queen, she could focus on the loss of her Soulbound. A searing ache branded her heart and she struggled to halt the tears that threatened to spill over once more. She paced from one side of the clearing to the other, wringing her hands in agitation. Tor and Bels watched her in silence.

"Tor, I have to go back for him. We're too close to Mandar City. He could have been hurt. He could have been captured." She refused to consider that he might have been killed. *I'd know. Somehow. I'd know if he were dead.*

The hippogryphs shared a look. Bels stepped forward, her brown coat shining in the morning sunlight. "Sera," she said gently, "I'm not sure that it's safe for any of us to return to Lake Eyre. If the flock finds any of us, we're dead. And realistically, what could any of us do to help a dragon?"

"I can help him! I need to go to him! You don't understand!" She could feel herself turning hysterical but couldn't rein in her emotions any longer. "We're connected. I can't survive without him, nor could he without me. We need each other!"

Tor narrowed his eyes and scrutinised her. "Sera... what you're saying... is this about more than connecting to him with your power?"

She bit her lip and didn't answer.

Realisation slowly dawned on his face and he said, "Tell me truthfully, have you been Soulbound to one another?"

She remained mute and studied the ground. A hiss of surprise came from Bels while he cocked his head and contemplated her.

"Well. This is... unusual." Turning his head sharply, he said, "Bels, we have to help her return to him."

The bay stamped her feet and spat out, "That is unnatural. No dragon should bind himself to a human. Not to mention, it is too dangerous to go back."

Sera took a deep breath and addressed both the hippogryphs. "I don't expect either of you to help me more than you already have. I want you to stay safe. I will return on my own and find him. I'm a Tracker. I'm good at finding lost mythics."

A shout in the distance interrupted their discussion and made all three freeze.

"That sounded like a human voice," Bels commented, throwing an accusatory glance towards Sera.

"We should check it out," suggested Tor, subtly adjusting his wings to disrupt the daggers the female hippogryph glared at Sera.

With a swish of her tail, she replied, "I'll go."

He bowed his head. "I'll stay here with Sera. Stay safe."

The bay hippogryph tucked her wings close to her sides and cantered east, melting into the trees.

Once she had travelled out of hearing, Tor turned to Sera. "I have to ask: do you know why the humans would have travelled this deep into the ranges?"

Frowning, Sera considered the question. "The only reasons I can think of, is they are tracking a rogue, or, perhaps... they could be searching for me?" Silently counting on her fingers, she said, "I've been gone about ten days, so maybe this is a search party?"

A flare of hope bloomed in her chest with the thought of returning to the safety of her home. To return to her father. A sick feeling burned away her momentary happiness and replaced it with the memories of her time with Arius. He had saved her life. He had taught her about the magic and the truth of the real world, not the fabricated one she had grown up thinking she knew.

He is my dragon. My Soulbound. I won't abandon him.

Torn between the beckoning comfort of her old life and the promise of the possibilities of her new life, she sat down, tormented. Craving an escape from her confused thoughts, she closed her eyes and sent her consciousness out. Bright spots flared all around her as the veil lifted and revealed the life that hummed through the earth. The lights of the insects and rodents were dwarfed by the swirling warmth of Tor's aura. Stretching further away from her body, she ignored the sparks of the small animals until she found Bels' life force hiding in thick underbrush along with that of five humans. Gently probing, she didn't recognise the first two auras she encountered. The third was familiar to her but she couldn't place the female. The fourth human's soul glowed, beckoning to her.

Dad! Her heart cried out to be with her father. She wished he could hear her thoughts the way her dragon could. *Dad will understand. If I go to him, he will call off the search and let me track down Arius.*

The last human's aura blazed into her mind's eye. The sickening feeling that accompanied it told her the owner's name as quickly as if she had seen him with her own eyes. Steel bands squeezed the air from her lungs as she thought his name.

Tyler.

CHAPTER THIRTY-FOUR

HER MIND WAS MADE up. Regardless of her or her father's wishes, Tyler would control the situation and have her returned to Mandar City.

I'll never be allowed to search for Arius if they take me back. I can't let them find me.

Distantly, she heard Tor calling her name urgently. Sadly, she began to withdraw her consciousness away from her father and back to her body. Shaking, she went to stand up but collapsed back to the ground, exhausted.

Panting, she looked up into the concerned face of Tor. "I heard you call my name, is everything okay?"

"I'm fine," he said. "You've been gone for a while and I know how that ended last time. I wanted to make sure you weren't going to faint for half a day."

"I'm getting stronger," she grunted as she forced herself to her feet, using his offered wing to balance. "Damn it," she huffed as she shuffled forward.

"What's the matter?"

"With everything that's happened, I didn't think about my backpack. It's got my food and survival kit in it. It must have been lost in the lake when we fell."

Tor made a conciliatory noise in his throat and said, "Allow me to fetch you some food and water." He stayed in step with her as she made her way towards the chuckling stream.

She rolled her eyes. "I'm not some damsel who needs to be waited on. I can find my own food and water."

He chuckled. "Yes, yes, I know, you're a fearsome Tracker who is Soulbound to a dragon. You're the last person who needs my help. But, please, allow me to be a gentleman, just this once. Forgive me for saying, but you do appear weakened."

"Yeah, well, no sleep for twenty-four hours and constantly fighting for survival will do that to a person," she grumbled as they arrived at the creek's edge.

"Which is precisely why you should let me fetch you something to eat."

"Fine." She thumped to the mossy ground in defeat. She cupped her hands in the creek and drank deeply. Tor disappeared briefly before returning with some watercress. "Thank you," she said, accepting the leafy plant gratefully.

"You're welcome." He nudged her shoulder kindly. "I can catch some fish for you if you'd like?"

"I would love some fish, but I can't eat it raw, and I don't think a fire is a good idea with the search party so close."

"Good point. So, you've chosen not to return to them?"

"Tor, you know I can't leave Arius. As tempting as it is to return to my old life, I can't go back. I have to find him."

The grey hippogryph bowed his head. "I understand."

Bels returned soon after and reported that five humans were sweeping the area a few ridges away and another team were at the base of the Mandar Ranges. She had also heard a strange whirring noise in the distance that she couldn't identify. After a short but passionate discussion, where Sera argued that she could take care of herself for

the short time it would take them to find food and shelter
for the night, the two of them left her alone.

The fatigue that she'd pushed back all morning had
settled into her bones. She lay down in the clearing and
allowed her eyes to drift shut. As exhausted as she was,
she couldn't stop her thoughts racing away from her.
Worry for her dragon, her father and her life, all whirled
through her mind. The tangle of stories shared with her
by the dragons played on repeat as she tried to unravel
the truth. The claim that she had some say in the future
of their world was a wonderfully impossible idea. However, the vision that alleged that her father wasn't Allen
was a hard pill to swallow. Unable to relax, she lay still
and focused on her breathing. Settling into a meditative
state, she listened to the birds calling to one another,
announcing the impending end of another day. The trees
rustled and the creek sang over the stones. The voices of
the search party had faded away as they headed in the
opposite direction.

She sank deeper into her meditation and stopped pure-
ly listening to her surroundings. She cast her mind out
and felt the tiny minds of the ants marching past her
resting form, intent on their purpose of finding food
for their queen. Pushing further away from herself, she
noticed the little honeyeater that was flitting between
flowers near her head, blissfully unaware of her presence.
As her power grew stronger, this exercise became almost restful, like stretching after a training session. Not
wanting to exhaust herself further, she began to retreat
into her mind but hesitated when an unexpected sense
of unease stole over her. There was a strange void to her
right. She could sense the two hippogryphs further away
to her left and other small creatures darting through the

underbrush between them, but there was a bubble of emptiness approaching from the opposite direction.

Abruptly, a foreign consciousness brushed against hers, immobilising her body, and bringing with it an impression of decay and the stench of rotting flesh. Her eyes snapped open and she stared in horror at the monster that appeared before her. The head and bust of a woman with taloned claws for legs and the wings of a vulture.

A harpy.

The lank strings of black hair fell from her head and covered her bony breast. The oily feathers appeared to ooze black blood that dripped to the ground as she stalked forwards. Her skinny arms were raised aggressively, thin fingers outstretched towards Sera with claws tipping each nail. At odds with the grotesque figure of her body, the harpy's face was angular and beautiful, in a terrible way. The tips of her ears were pointed, and purple irises filled the almond-shaped eyes, giving her face an almost cat-like appearance.

Sera went to recoil in horror but was unable to move. The harpy's magic wrapped around her body, trapping her and leaving her gagged.

"Hush." The mythic's gravelly voice was the sound of ice scraping against rock. "If you struggle, you'll just make it worse for yourself."

Leaning down, she grabbed Sera's hand and examined the palm closely, twisting it as she examined the faint golden line that was the only sign of where Arius had cut her. The claws dug into her skin and she struggled to scream, but only a choked garble came out.

"Well now, isn't this interesting?" The harpy's voice grated as she tugged Sera's shirt down to reveal the matching scar over her heart.

The action left her feeling violated as the creature placed a taloned foot on her chest then inserted her skeletal finger into Sera's mouth. Drawing a line on the inside of her cheek with her claw, the harpy pulled the bloodied nail out and sucked it. Her pupils dilated until the black filled her eyes and she bared her fangs in a terrifying smile.

"What a wonderful development. My employer will be pleased. Now, my dear, you will be coming with me. I know, I know, I'm sure this is all very confusing for you. What you must understand is that these mythics you have befriended, they have lied to you. They are trying to instigate another war. And we don't want that now, do we? Your dragon knows that you are more powerful than you realise, especially now that he has tricked you into being Soulbound to him. He, and your hippogryph friends, are trying to turn you away from your people."

That's not true! She wanted to scream at the harpy, but more than that, she wanted to plunge Firinne into her lying mouth.

"I can see you don't believe me. The thing is, you've been brainwashed. Ever heard of Stockholm Syndrome? Of course you have. That's what your precious dragon has done. He took you against your will, but he was kind to you. He pretended to care for you, all the while feeding you the lies that will pave the way for a new war. I'm here to save you from him. From this path of destruction that he would lead you down. Come with me quietly and I will return you safely to Mandar City where you can report to the MRO."

Sera sensed the precise moment the harpy eased her magic off, and she wasted no time in lunging for Firinne and sweeping it up to cut into the harpy's flesh. Before it reached its target, the knife halted mid-strike and the staghorn handle burned her hand. Crying out, she dropped the blade and the magic gripped her once again in its harsh embrace.

"Tsk, tsk, my dear. That is no way to treat your saviour. My employer asked for you to be returned to him alive, but he failed to mention in what condition. After that outburst, I think you need a little reminder of your manners."

The harpy picked up Firinne and placed the sharp tip against Sera's arm. The magic held her body still as the knife sliced into her forearm. Sera gritted her teeth as tears silently dripped down her face.

"There, that should do it." She stepped back to admire her handiwork as blood trickled from the wound. "There's more where that came from if you try anything else," she warned.

Tossing the knife away into the nearest bush, the harpy lifted Sera easily into her arms and leapt into the air. The stench of decay that clung to the mythic like a cloak made her gag, but the magic still paralysed her. Black blood splattered onto her skin with each beat of the harpy's wings. Air rushed over them as they turned east and headed towards the city.

The harpy leered at Sera as they flew and she said, "It's time to go home, Seraphina."

Epilogue

THE WOMAN HE HAD left chained inside the padded cell groaned as the iron bit into her skin. President Kaesus closed the heavy door tightly behind him, tapping a code into the keypad to lock it. He blinked as he allowed his eyes to adjust to the bright fluorescent lights. Striding along the uninterrupted hallway, his footsteps echoed through the empty space. The crisp, white walls lent the prison a clinical feel. His blood hummed; he felt revitalised after his visit to the broken woman. Reaching the end of the corridor he swiped his security pass through the access panel, keyed in his six-digit code, and walked through the armoured doors as they hissed open. Stepping into the cool night air, he pulled his blazer closer around him. He stalked away from the building that housed only his captive and made his way towards the bright lights of the main cell block.

Passing through a gate flanked by barbed wire fences he crossed the dark exercise yard. The fence surrounded the entire Iniques Rehabilitation Centre. Electrified mesh stretched overhead to create a domed cage to ensure that no flighted creatures could escape. The main building was massive as it was required to house all manner of prisoners, both human and mythics. His phone buzzed angrily in his pocket, its glow lighting his piercing icy-blue eyes.

Touching the screen, he answered curtly, "Yes."

When he heard the update from the scratchy voice of the harpy, his mouth curled into a cruel grin.

"Good. Take her straight to the drop-off. I'll meet you there."

Swiping his access card once more, he entered the main building. Ignoring the many doors lining the hall, he made his way to the front desk. A head of sleek black hair peeked over the counter as the President frowned at the strange sentry behind the desk.

"You're new."

"Good evening, Mr President, sir." The Hunter-turned-prison-guard jumped to his feet and snapped to attention. "I'm Hunter Jun. Hunter Baxter is away on leave, so I'm taking over during his absence."

"I haven't seen you around before. Have you been given the rundown on the standard procedure for my visits?" President Kaesus hated change, particularly when it wasn't orchestrated by him.

"Yes, sir. I have signed the NDA, and I understand that if I happen to see or hear anything while you're onsite, which I'm sure I won't, I am not to interrupt or to share that information with anyone, on pain of death."

"Good." He crossed his arms. "How long will Baxter be away for?"

"He's only away for a week, Mr President."

"Fine. Leave a message for him to contact me as soon as he returns."

"Yes, sir."

The President's eyes slid over to the TV that hung on the wall in the corner of the room. The local news was broadcasting the latest revelation on the missing Tracker case.

The journalist onscreen declared, "President Malcolm Kaesus has committed to sending his private helicopter to search for the missing Tracker, Seraphina Azura, after her father reported her missing six days ago."

Jun followed his gaze and cocked his head. "No word yet on Tracker Sera?"

He hesitated before replying, "No, no word from the rescue team yet."

"Shame. She seemed like a talented Tracker. Odd that she would get lost." Jun shrugged. "Not my business anyway. Can I help you with anything else tonight, Mr President, sir?"

"No, my business is finished here," he said and stalked out of the IRC.

His driver and bodyguards waited at his black armoured car, one of only a few that had been commissioned after the Mythic War. Sliding into the backseat, he instructed his team to take him to Grave's Point, an old lookout on a hill above Mandar City. The dirt road was corrugated and the going slow, but that meant the chances of anyone else being here at this time of night was slim. Once they arrived, he allowed his bodyguards to sweep the area before requesting that they remain at the car while he enjoyed the view alone. Grabbing his briefcase, he left his entourage in the car park, jogged up the stairs and followed the winding boardwalk to the viewing platform.

From there, the bright lights of the city were laid out like a miniature galaxy before him. Turning away from the vista he peered up the hill, scanning the star-studded sky. An awkward form appeared out of the dark and flapped towards him. The harpy and her human cargo alighted on the wooden deck of Grave's Point and she dropped the young woman's body to the ground at his feet.

"Here she is, alive as requested. Fun fact, she is Soulbound to the dragon. Now, where's my reward?"

Pulling his phone out, he replied, "They're Soulbound? In that case, you haven't completed the task. I need them both."

She snarled and raised a clawed hand, threatening to strike.

He grabbed her by the throat and opened his contacts list, his finger hovering over the screen. "All it will take is one phone call and you'll be reunited with your clutch. Or you could lose them forever. It's your choice."

Feathers bristling, the harpy lowered her talons sullenly.

"Good. Now finish the job and I'll give you back your family."

The harpy flew off and President Kaesus eyed the blood-stained girl with distaste. She groaned and rolled stiffly to her feet now the harpy's magic had lifted.

He plastered a smile on his face. "Tracker Seraphina! I'm so thankful that the harpy found you!" He embraced her tightly as she stood frozen in shock. "It is so good to finally meet you." He stepped back and held her at arms-length. "Has anyone ever told you that you have your father's eyes?" His grip tightened for a moment, then he released her.

"I don't understand what's happening," she rasped out.

"You've had a massive shock, Seraphina. I know about the dragon, but don't worry, you're not in trouble. I know it wasn't your fault. Dragons are excellent at manipulating the truth into some twisted version that suits their ambitions."

"That's not true. Arius didn't lie to me." She looked between him and the forest at their back as if calculating her chances of escape.

"So, his name is Arius? I'm sure you believed Arius had your best interests at heart. Let me explain everything to you. It will all make sense soon." He spoke in soothing tones as he opened his briefcase and withdrew a needle. "You are hurt, Seraphina. I'll just inject you with this Vital Heal and you'll feel much better."

"No." She swayed on her feet and held her hands up. "I don't want you to give me anything."

"It's all going to be okay," he coaxed as he gripped her arm and pulled the sleeve back.

"Stop it," she whimpered and feebly tried to push his hands away.

Swiftly, he injected the serum into her veins and shoved her against the handrail. He placed his head next to hers, his lips whispering against her ear, "That injection was a special mix of my own. It eliminates memories and replaces them with whatever I tell you. What's going to happen now is, you're going to walk towards Mandar City until you can't walk any further. When you are discovered, starving and dehydrated, you will not remember anything from the moment that dragon took you. You were out camping and hunting deer when you fell and hit your head. When you woke up you managed to survive in the wild and made your way home alone. You won't remember the harpy, you won't remember this meeting. And you won't remember your precious dragon!"

He spat the last sentence at her and violently flung her body away in disgust. She stumbled and fell to the ground, staring up at him with fear in her wide, blue eyes, the loose strands of her auburn hair tumbling around her face.

"No," she whispered, terror lacing her words.

He smirked at her. "It's for the greater good, Seraphina. Sometimes, one must make difficult decisions to secure the future of Mandar. One day you might have to make a similar choice."

He marched back to his car, leaving Sera hunched over and sobbing as the memories of her dragon trickled away with each tear that soaked into the earth.

LINKS

If you enjoyed A Dragon's Mind, please leave a review:

https://altippett.com/rl/2079996

Read A Dragon's Body, Book Two in The MINATH Chronicles:

https://altippett.com/rl/2079997

Claim your FREE short story when you subscribe to my monthly newsletter:

https://altippett.com/latest-updates/subscribe/

Get to know me by visiting:

https://altippett.com

Or by following my socials:

https://facebook.com/altippettauthor

https://instagram.com/a_l_tippett_author

https://tiktok.com/@altippett

https://bookbub.com/profile/a-l-tippett

https://goodreads.com/altippett

Acknowledgements

Firstly, I want to thank you. Yes, you there, holding this book. Whether you are reading these pages on your Kindle, phone, tablet or if you've got your hands wrapped around the spine of a paperback... I want to say a heartfelt thank you for reading this story. I hope you loved reading it as much as I loved creating it.

If you enjoyed this book, please consider leaving a review. But please remember to be kind. I poured a part of my soul into these pages and, while my brain knows that it won't be everyone's cup of tea (and that's okay), my heart craves acceptance. I'm always happy for readers to reach out to me with constructive feedback; if you have any suggestions on improvements for future books please head to my website to get in touch.

And don't forget to grab your copy of book two: *A Dragon's Body.* If you thought Sera was struggling in this book, just wait until you see what's in store for her in the next one!

I want to sincerely thank the professionals who helped make *A Dragon's Mind* the best story that it could be. In particular, thanks to my editor Sheryl Lee who offered helpful advice and guidance that was so appreciated by a newbie author like myself. She taught me many things through the editing process and I'm sure I will continue to learn from her!

A massive thank you to my new designer, MiblArt, for the stunning cover.

I want to give a big shout-out to the lovely Kealie of KKP Photography in Mackay. She donated her time and skills to give me a professional photo shoot for my author portrait after she learned I was struggling with postnatal depression. Kealie, you don't know how much you cheered me up that day, thank you.

Many thanks to my wonderful beta readers, Kara and Claire. Your feedback was very helpful and *A Dragon's Mind* is a better story because of you. Thanks also go to Laura, for always lending an ear for me to bounce ideas off. Your friendship means the world to me.

A thousand thank yous to all the family members and friends who have offered support for my first foray into the daunting world of writing and self-publishing a novel. I feel so fortunate to have you all in my life. A special mention to the members of 20Booksto50k® for their willingness to share the details of their journey up the mountain.

Last, but not least, thank you to the seven most important people in my life.

Mum and Dad, you amaze me. Your strength of character and free spirits have guided me to where I am today. You have always inspired me to take the road less travelled, and I am so thankful for that. Love you uttmasaba.

Madonna and Paul, you're the best in-laws a girl could ask for. Thank you for always offering words of encouragement and a kick up the bum when I get side-tracked. I love that you are almost as excited as I am about this story! Love you both lots.

To my children, you bring me so much joy. It's because of you that I decided to take a chance on this writing caper. Thank you for inspiring me to be a better person. I hope one day, when you're a bit older (and hopefully not still waking me up every night) you'll look at your mum's achievements and be proud. I love you both beyond words.

Thank you, Mitchell, for always being the wind at my back, and not the spit in my face. You never fail to offer your support in all of my hair-brained schemes, and I will forever be grateful for that. You're my number one. I love you.

Fly fierce, strike strong.

April xo

ABOUT THE AUTHOR

I was born in the South Island of New Zealand before my family and I moved to Australia when I was two years old. We lived on a yacht for a few years and travelled along the east coast of Aussie and across the Pacific Ocean to New Caledonia. My parents home-schooled us while we sailed the seas until we bought a house on the Sunshine Coast in Queensland. I finally got to go to "real-school" and loved it – I couldn't understand why we had weekends (because, according to my husband, I'm just a big nerd).

Shortly before beginning high school, we moved north to a rural property near Mackay. The big draw card was that I could finally buy my own horse, a dream I'd had since I was a little girl. On my first day at my new school, I met a boy on the bus who teased me mercilessly; nine years later we were married!

I started writing my first fantasy novel when I was twelve but abandoned it after deciding that being an author wasn't a "real" job and therefore not worth pursuing. After completing my secondary schooling, my parents encouraged me to experience the real world before committing to a university degree. So, I applied to be a rider in a travelling horse show! Unfortunately, I wasn't successful so instead I did the complete opposite and got a job as an insurance broker. I worked in insurance for seven years before leaving to start a family.

My husband and I have now welcomed two children into our lives – a pigeon pair. I feel very fortunate to be able to stay at home and care for them whilst my husband works away. It's tricky finding the time to write with two small children but, as they say, where there's a will, there's a way! I can't wait to get started on my next book am looking forward to sharing many more stories with you!

Printed in Great Britain
by Amazon

42998660R00121